ATTACK THE GEEK

MICHAEL R. UNDERWOOD

PRAISE FOR MICHAEL R. UNDERWOOD

"If *Buffy* hooked up with *Doctor Who* while on board the Serenity, this book would be their lovechild. In other words, *Geekomancy* is full of epic win."

– Marie Lu, author of the Legend trilogy, on *Geekomancy*

"Michael R. Underwood just keeps getting better and better. We need more urban fantasy like this."

– Seanan McGuire, New York Times bestselling author of *Discount Armageddon*, on *Celebromancy*

"This is truly a unique spin on the typical Urban Fantasy story and one of the most genuinely fun stories I have read in a long time."

– KristenD, Bitten by Books, on *Attack the Geek*

"Come for the geeky world and fun storyline, stay for the fabulous characters, relationships, and action. I thoroughly enjoyed the whole series; I simply loved *Hexomancy*. I commend it for your reading pleasure. Seriously, pre-order today."

– Joe's Geek Fest, on *Hexomancy*

"Heroes, villains, and a world like no other."

– Joe's Geek Fest on *Shield & Crocus*

" . . .a bright and exciting space opera in the cosmic comic book style of Marvel's *Guardians of the Galaxy*. In a galaxy that has been dominated by the mollusk-like Vsenk for a thousand years, three treasure hunters stumble across an artifact that will shake the foundations of an entire empire . . .Underwood's prose is brisk and funny without ever sacrificing his skilled sf world building. Highly recommended for fans of action-packed space opera and anyone else looking for a fun and fast-paced read.

– Booklist (Starred Review), on Annihilation Aria

"In this entertaining space opera from Underwood (the Genrenauts series), a married couple—one an affable archaeologist from Earth who was accidentally transported across the universe with no way home, the other a warrior woman from a devastated alien culture who utilizes songs to enhance her combat skills—becomes embroiled in a mess of galactic proportions after they "liberate" a dangerous artifact from a long-lost temple . . .This is a rollicking good time."

– Publisher's Weekly, on Annihilation Aria

"*Annihilation Aria* is the found family space opera you've been waiting for."

– Adam Rakunas, author of Philip K. Dick Award-finalist Windswept

"*The Younger Gods* is a solid urban fantasy with an interesting premise and characters you can't help but get invested in."

– Bibliotropic

"This is fun . . .Readers will be looking forward to Leah and company's next trip to a story world."

– Library Journal, on Genrenauts: The Shootout Solution

"This is one of those high concepts so irresistible, you can't believe no one has come up with it before. This first installment is a rollicking exploration of western tropes, with hints of a larger conspiracy afoot. Underwood has plans for a lot more of these, and I can't wait to read them."

– Joel Cunningham, Barnes & Noble Sci-Fi & Fantasy Blog,
on Genrenauts: The Shootout Solution

"A Tardis of a novella, *The Shootout Solution* is packed full of ideas . . . The possibilities are endless . . . Tor.com continues to blaze a bookish trail in terms of both originality and diversity. More like this, please."

– Geek Syndicate, on Genrenauts: The Shootout Solution

"*The Shootout Solution* is Genre blending fun."

– Fangirl Nation

"A clever, exciting, and seriously fun twist on portal fantasy that sends a geeky stand-up comedian into the Wild West. Sign me up to be a Genrenaut, too!"

– Delilah S. Dawson, NYT-bestselling author of *Star Wars: Phasma*

"I have this sinking feeling that the Genrenauts series, with its raucous meta-commentary upon the stories of pop culture, is going to say important things that I might not be clever enough to catch the first time around because I'm too busy enjoying the books."

– Howard Tayler, Hugo Award Winner and creator of *Schlock Mercenary*

"My favorite new TV show of 2015 isn't on TV, it's in the pages of Mike Underwood's Genrenauts. Deeply funny and creative, shrewdly insightful, and thrillingly paced, every pop culture diehard will want to keep living vicariously through the characters in this series."

– Matt Wallace, Hugo Award winner and author of the Savage Rebellion and Sin du Jour series

"*Born to the Blade* is the best Fantasy Epic NOT on TV"

– Inverse

"a complex and fascinating world that is filled with cool shit."

– Liz Bourke for Tor.com, on *Born to the Blade*

2nd edition
Copyright © 2014, 2022 by Michael R. Underwood

For rights inquiries, contact info@morhaimliterary.com
ISBN: 9780998060668 (Paperback)
        9780998060675 (ebook)

Cover by Deranged Doctor Design (derangeddoctordesign.com)
Also available in audiobook

First edition by Simon & Schuster Pocket Star Books April 2014
1st edition ISBN 9781476757780

MORE BY MICHAEL R. UNDERWOOD

The Ree Reyes Geeky Urban Fantasy Series
Geekomancy
Celebromancy
Attack the Geek
Hexomancy

Genrenauts
#0 -The Data Disruption
#1 -The Shootout Solution
#2 - The Absconded Ambassador
#3 -The Cupid Reconciliation
#4 - The Substitute Sleuth
#5&6 - The Failed Fellowship
#7 - The Wasteland War

The Space Operas
Annihilation Aria

Other Books
Shield and Crocus

The Younger Gods

Born to the Blade
(with Malka Older, Cassandra Khaw, and Marie Brennan)

There's Something About Saturdays

NOW

A hundred fists hammered at the sturdy wood of the thick front door at Grognard's Grog and Games. Ree pressed her back against the door, her boots sliding on the smooth floor of the concrete, failing to find a good grip. The shop was a total wreck—games, cards, figures, and props scattered everywhere, drinks spilled across the bar, tables upended and shattered. Ree wanted to think that the gnomes couldn't make it much worse, but the "getting eaten alive" part banished that thought pretty fast.

"What the fuck has gotten into those little guys?" Ree asked. Pearson's sewer gnomes were already more like ghouls than the helpful creatures in *David the Gnome* or the curious tinkerers from *D&D*, but this was a whole new level of aggro.

Eastwood stood beside her, leaning into the door with one shoulder, cuts and bruises scored across his face and hands.

"Don't know, but we can't hold out long like this. And if they get in, we're *bantha pudu*."

Ree could feel the scraping and scratching at the door, then a louder *thud*.

That was no gnome. Ree took a millisecond to consider what else might be out there, but it didn't really matter, since it probably wanted them dead just as much as the tiny creatures.

"How we doing back there?" Ree shouted to the back room.

"A short while longer, sad to say!" Drake answered, his voice hoarse.

Ree cursed under her breath. "We're not made of time out here. Either the gnomes have made themselves a battering ram, or there's a cave Troll out there!"

"It wouldn't be a cave Troll. They hate the smell down here. Sewer Troll, maybe," Eastwood said.

"Thanks, Mr. Monster Manual," Ree said, short temper unleashing the full power of her snark. "How does this help us not get murderated?"

Beat.

"It doesn't," Eastwood admitted.

"Then I don't need to know. Hurry up, guys!" Ree shouted again.

Eastwood nudged her. "Get to a weapon. I've got this."

"That's ridiculous. The door will cave in as soon as I move."

"Trust me. We need to be ready."

"I trust you, but I still think it's ridiculous."

"I'll take it," Eastwood said, pushing her away from the door.

What the fuck is it about Saturdays? Ree asked herself as she felt the door splintering behind her.

CHAPTER ONE

Three Hours Earlier

"How the hell am I supposed to trust you!" Ree flung her hands in the air, ready to give up her dinner break and get back to work just so she could walk away from this ridiculousness.

She stood at a tall table facing Eastwood, her onetime mentor in all things fantastical. But their partnership had lasted about as long as a Las Vegas marriage once she discovered that he was making deals with devils.

He was trying to atone, but humility was apparently not part of his penance.

Eastwood kept his voice level, seizing the person-who-shouts-is-losing-the-argument high ground. "This is major league magic, Ree. It comes with a price."

"But seriously, puppies?"

"You wanted ideas. I heard this from someone on r/WeirdMagic."

Ree scoffed. "Your first mistake was going to Reddit for advice. Your second mistake was mentioning anything that possibly leads to puppies getting hurt."

"I can make it painless. Unless you think we can steal Death's scythe and trundle down to the underworld ourselves like *The Middleman*." Eastwood crossed his arms, digging in.

Ree couldn't see a downside to that plan. "Why not?"

"Because Death outclasses the Duke, and we only survived last time because I managed to think ahead."

"Wait. Who was it that dropped trou and shouted the Duke out of town, again? There's got to be like fifty quick-escape artifacts out in the world, right? We sneak in, stun or distract Captain Hoodie, grab the goods, and then scurry away on a getaway gadget. Next stop, reunion town!"

"So you think you're hot *shit*, now?" Eastwood replied. "The Duke almost killed us both. And if we put him in a position to team up with Death, it won't matter if we do get Branwen out of Hell, because we'll all be headed straight back there ourselves, faster than Fox can cancel a new SF show."

Ree narrowed her eyes at the older geek.

Fuck it. All of the hero-ing in the world wouldn't erase what he'd done to those kids.

She turned and made her way to the office to grab her apron and get back to work. They were never going to see eye to eye on this. The only solutions Eastwood offered on how to get her mom (aka his girlfriend) back from her tenure in Hell as the guest of the Thrice-Retconed Duke of Pwn involved a lively stroll through the Dark Side.

When she'd met him, Eastwood had been collecting the souls of teen suicides to trade to the Duke for her mom's freedom, and would have succeeded if not for Ree, who was, like any person not grief-wracked, opposed to sacrificing kids to a demon. And anytime she suggested an alternative breakout plan, Eastwood dismissed it out of hand, usually not bothering to explain why. Which meant they kept circling the issue, never getting anywhere.

Tying her apron back on, Ree toggled her brain back to work mode.

Saturday night at Grognard's Grog and Games meant three things: *V:TES* tournament, half-price Jaeger, and Grognard getting morose.

Ree Reyes (Strength 10, Dexterity 14, Stamina 12, Will 18, IQ 16, Charisma 15—Geek 7 / Barista 3 / Screenwriter 3 / Gamer Girl 2 / Geekomancer 2) had noticed that there was something about Saturdays that got to Grognard like an itch in that one place on your back that was physiologically impossible to scratch without help. So that night, like most Saturdays, she tried to keep her head down and stay out of his way. Her boss was almost unbelievably permissive with her whacky urban fantasy schedule, which more than made up for his eccentricities. And the employee discount made her hero-ing far more affordable.

The bar section of the shop was half-full, four booths and two tables crammed full with players wheeling, dealing, drinking, and thinking over games of *Vampire: The Eternal Struggle (V:TES for short)*. During the day, most of the action was on the other side of the store, where rows of comics, cards, and collectibles tempted customers of all stripes—Grognard's was occult shop, hangout bar for magicians, and game store all in one.

Ree took a shortcut through the store section rather than navigating through the tables, a tray of drinks and food balanced expertly on her shoulder. Ree Reyes was in her full bartender costume: black jeans, black T-shirt over black undershirt, her shoulder-length hair tied back and held up with a pair of ebony chopsticks, and around one eye, drawn-on sunburst markings taken straight out of *Dollhouse*'s "Epitaph Two."

After a few months, customers had come to expect the facial art, and it was a fun challenge. So before she knew it, drawing on her face had become part of her pre-work ritual, except on days when she'd come straight from fighting monsters or tromping through the sewers, which was more often than you might think.

Ree set her tray down on an empty table and passed out Redheaded Sisters, mozzarella sticks, and pints of Grognard's Vorpal Bunny IPA. Back at the bar, the titular Grognard (Strength 14, Dexterity 10, Stamina 15, IQ 15, Will 18, Charisma 10—Geek 7 / Collector 4 / Geekomancer 3 / Brewmaster 5) kept an eye on the room, mixing drinks without having to look down. Callused and gnarled hands worked on autopilot while the bald brewmaster stared off into the distance the way he always did on Saturdays.

Grognard snapped back to attention when asked a question by Ree's least-favorite member of the local Steampunk community, the self-appointed "Lieutenant" Abigail Wickham.

Abigail Wickham (Strength 13, Dexterity 14, Stamina 12, Will 8, IQ 14, Charisma 16—Old Money 4 / Mean Girl 3 / Model 2 / Blogger 2 / Steampunk 2) was a walking catalog page straight out of *Vogue*: Steampunk.

Three-paned goggles, by Dr. Einsteinium = $299

Butterfly Cog hair pin, by Lady Jaydite = $79

Resist! **earrings**, by Francesca Riviera de la Vega = $329

Whalebone, jade, and ivory-boned bustier Shackles, by Zenia = $899

Functional Pneumatic Needler gun, by Dr. Einsteinium = $1,999

Crimson-to-black asymmetrical Bustle Skirt, by Francesa Riviera de la Vega = $249

Custom brown duster, by Lobelia Judgehammer = $1,499

Custom thigh-high leather boots, by Made for Walking = $499

Every piece of gear had a story, a relationship, but even while wearing the work of a dozen master craftswomen and -men, Wickham still made it all about herself. She collected awesome craftspeople like they were Pokémon, their accomplishments and capabilities turned to her ends.

Wickham had made her distaste for the handiwork of Ree's friends Priya, as well as Drake Winters, abundantly, self-righteously clear. Therefore, Ree made a point of never bothering with Wickham if she could avoid it, so she walked straight by the "Lieutenant" and returned to her duties, making a barback sweep to clear glasses and plates. Grognard refused to hire actual barbacks, instead relying on Ree to clear tables. It usually wasn't a problem, even on Saturdays. Mostly it meant that she wore through a pair of insoles in a month.

On the upside, the extra runs gave her a chance to check in on the games. She'd played *V:TES* back in the day, usually after school and on weekends, when there had been time for a three-hour chunk of deal-making, face-pounding, and sudden but inevitable betrayals. It wasn't quite as much fun as LARPing *Vampire*, but it took a hell of a lot less prep time, and cards cost less than makeup and costumes.

Uncle Joe, a Grognard's regular, was handily in control of his game, his Nosferatu stealthy enough to make him a difficult target, leading the other players to take swipes at one another. On the surface, Uncle Joe looked like any one of a million milquetoast white guys: balding, heavy-set, pale complexion, topped off with a collection of sweater-vests. But when it came to card-flopping, he was a Monte Carlo shark.

Eastwood sat in the nearest booth, in Master Geekomancer mode, though like everyone else, he was observing the No Magic rule that applied to all tournaments.

Eastwood had gone from scruffy hero to full-on 90s-antihero-on-the-redemption-crusade since last October, doing penance by cavorting around Pearson night and day, thereby proving that the superheroes who patrolled actively were, in fact, ridiculous.

Eastwood (Strength 11, Dexterity 14, Stamina 14, IQ 18, Will 18, Charisma 7—Geek 8, Astral Cowboy 4 / Geekomancer 5 / Thunderbolt 1) looked like he hadn't slept in a week; he had deep circles under his eyes, and his beard was a full order more scraggly than usual.

Ree wondered if there was a connection between Eastwood's strung-out-itude and Grognard's especially grumpy Saturdays.

Maybe it has something to do with Mom, Ree wondered. After ditching her husband and daughter, Ree's mom had gone back to her Geekomantic ways and shacked up with Eastwood before dying under mysterious circumstances, which, as noted, had prompted Eastwood's rampage through the Dark Side in an effort to get her back.

Ree chewed on that mystery while she cleaned the tables and checked the games. Three of them were in endgame, but the rest might stretch on for another couple of hours. The night was young.

Hauling a full tray back to the bar, Ree hip-checked her way into the back, where she dropped off the tray beside the dishwasher. Elbow-deep in suds, Drake was hard at work, scrubbing a huge glass jug that Grognard used for brewing. The room smelled of soap and sweat.

Ree had been working for Grognard since the start of November, but Drake had volunteered his services after a cluster-fuck of a night where the pair of them had lost Grognard's traveling cart and several pony kegs of beer during a not-so-random monster attack in the sewer.

Drake's sleeves were rolled up to his biceps, giving him a more decidedly working-class look, as his jacket was hung up on the coat rack in Grognard's office. His suspenders hung down and back over his pants. The overall effect was deliciously retro blue collar-y.

A man out of time, Drake Winters (Strength 12, Dexterity 15, Stamina 13, IQ 16, Will 15, Charisma 15—Inventor 5 / Gentleman 2 / Steampunk 6 / Fae-Touched 3) was just barely taller than Ree, his riding boots set aside for the long dishwashing shifts. His short sandy-blond hair slicked to his forehead with the sheen of sweat and steam, and his hands were so pruny, they qualified him to be a backup dancer for the California Raisins.

"Good day, Ms. Ree. How are the games proceeding?" he asked, setting the jug down on the counter and wiping the sweat from his brow.

"Eastwood and Uncle Joe are kicking ass, Shade has all of his opponents paranoid, and Talon had an elder on the table before anyone could blink."

Drake nodded politely, though as far as she could tell, he'd never played *V:TES* or any other CCG. He was a much older-school kind of geek, more about the gears and geegaws than the card-flopping and the fan-vidding. Which, coming from an entirely different dimension as he did, was entirely understandable.

"You doing all right back here? Need a drink?" Ree asked.

Drake chuckled, laughter brightening his already warm demeanor. "Strange that spending hours half-submerged in water and soap could leave a person dehydrated, but so it is. I would adore an iced tea or water, if it is not too much trouble."

What Ree wanted to do was to wink suggestively and take a page from Rogue and say something like, "For you, sugar, anything."

But since Drake was still dating one of her best friends, all she said was "Coming right up."

Ree got herself out of the situation before she could say something regretable, and went back out onto the bar floor.

Thou shalt not fuck with one of thy best friends' relationships, she told herself, a refrain she'd had to repeat countless times.

During Ree's brief stint as a screenwriter a few months back, superstar actress (and childhood crush) Jane Konrad had, upon observing her and Drake together, told her, *"And since he's no longer the competition, I might as well tell you that Drake is wild about you."*

Perhaps. But he was still with Priya, and when Ree had the ovaries to deal with the emotional roller coaster that came from seeing them together, they appeared to be perfectly happy. Which meant that she had to be a grown-up about it and deal.

Grognard caught her attention as she crossed his thousand-yard stare.

"Can't afford breaks for you to moon at Captain Dashing right now. I need you to stay on top of the tables."

And, of course, everyone knew about it but Drake. *Gods, kill me now and spare me the soap opera.*

It was about then that the lights went out.

CHAPTER TWO

Lightsaber Is My Nightlight

I was kidding! Ree said to herself. Drama was still preferable to death, no matter how gut-wrenching.

"Balls," said Grognard. Ree set her tray down on the bar that she knew was directly to her left, then reached into her apron for the penlight on her keychain.

The crowd started grumbling, which also had the effect of keeping her oriented.

"I'll get the breaker," Ree said, turning and walking back toward the office, hands out, since her penlight was barely up to the task of illuminating the door two feet in front of her.

Grognard huffed in the affirmative. "Everyone keep your shit together. It's just a breaker."

"My phone isn't working," said one of the players as Ree opened the door.

"We barely get signal down here on a good day. That's why I open up the Wi-Fi," Grognard explained with a tired voice.

"But I have a dedicated satellite signal with underground relays, and I'm not getting anything either," said Shade, Pearson's local '80s-New-Wave Cyberpunk Technomancer.

Curiouser and curiouser. Ree pawed her way to the fuse box and threw the breakers. Nothing happened. She did it again, and the breaker shot out a burst of sparks that lit the office for a split second like fireworks on Lunar New Year before going dark again.

Ree hopped back from the fuse box, steadying herself on the wall.

"Boss?" she called. The Saturday Suck was really outdoing itself this week.

"What was that?" Grognard said. She heard the door swing open, then felt a heavy presence beside her.

"I wouldn't do that," Ree said, reaching for her boss's arm as he moved past her.

Grognard brushed by and stopped in front of the fuse box. "What happened?"

"The fuse box gave off a shower of sparks. I suspect that we will not solve this problem easily," Drake said from the sinks.

"Let me take a look at it. With these boots, I'm as grounded as someone can get," he said.

There was a set of clicks, then another. No sparks, but no lights, either. Ree considered pulling out her lightsaber to use as a flare, but if it turned out that there was something hinky, she didn't want to run down its nostalgia battery too soon. In her time as a part of Pearson's magical underground, she'd learned that holding back the big guns kept you alive.

Grognard squinted at the fuse box, then sighed. "Okay, I'm calling it. Lock the register and help me lead people out the office exit."

There were two ways out of Grognard's—the big round front door that led out into the sewers of Pearson, and the employee entrance in the office, which led out and up into a mundane building.

"Got it," Ree said, heading to the bar area.

"Okay, everyone, we're going to have to close for the night," Grognard said loudly.

That prompted a round of boos, some grumbles, and a load of shuffling, as people collected themselves (and their cards) in the dark. Ree heard a glass fall and shatter on the floor, then got a whiff of beer. She heard more shuffling, like someone trying to clean up after themselves. *Le sigh.*

"Leave it; let's just get going. We're taking the office door, so just come with me, okay?" Ree kept talking to give the patrons something to home in on. "Last one out forfeits their entrance fee to the tourney, everyone else gets a refund."

The shuffling got a bit faster, and Ree held the door open.

"Incoming," Ree said over her shoulder. Then there was a loud *SMACK.*

Ree turned around to see the barkeep picking himself up off the floor.

"Hold that thought," Grognard said.

"What?" said one of the customers.

"Say what?" Ree echoed.

"Office door's warded." A moment later, her boss added, "And they're not my wards."

Uh-oh, Ree thought. The Occam's Razor answer of "malfunction" was losing ground to "sabotage" by the moment.

"What kind of wards?" asked Eastwood from halfway back in the group. There were sounds of jostling as he pushed through the crowd and walked by Ree, his heavy steps setting him apart from the other customers. Eastwood always walked like he was stomping bugs underheel. Maybe it was something left over from his time as an astral-projecting cowboy, as if he was trying to make up for the spurs he'd set aside years ago.

"Can't be sure from here. But when I tried to force the door, it hit me like a haymaker," Grognard said.

"Screw this. I'm out of here," one customer said, and then Ree heard a wave of steps and shoves as the assorted gamers and Geekomancers made their way to the sewer door.

Ree followed the customers out into the bar area, half out of curiosity and half to make sure no one swiped or broke something on the way out. Grognard had a handful of big-league artifacts that could cause some major damage if they fell into the wrong hands. Thankfully, most of them were locked away under glass.

The door to the sewers opened without incident, and most of the customers filed out, making their own light with props or simple spells, or they just dealt with the darkness—like Shade. But if *his* specs didn't have magical functions, Ree would eat her apron.

"Everybody out that wants out?" Ree asked to the remaining customers. Ree guessed there were two, maybe three left inside.

She didn't hear any other movement, so she hauled the huge circular door closed and secured it with the three warded locks. The locks' magics were specifically designed by Grognard to interconnect and support one another, and so far, she'd never had reason to doubt them.

"You can grab any seat you like," Ree said to the remaining customers. "I'll bring you some drinks, on the house."

She wove her way through the bar, relying on memory and touch to avoid the tables and chairs. She rummaged around behind the bar until she found several gas lanterns. Then, giving herself some light, she drew several pints of Critical Hit and headed back to the table. The customers left behind were Uncle Joe; Patricia Talon, the sword-maker; and Abigail Wickham. But Wickham accepted the draft with a nod, saving her biting wit for once. The trio started chatting about the interrupted games, and Ree headed back to the office to check on the door.

"Any luck?" she asked, a Maglite flashlight in hand.

"Nada," said Grognard. "I'll set out the rest of the lights. Sort the drawer into the safe and hang tight." At least she'd be able to catch up on her sleep this way.

"Got it," Ree said.

She'd just opened the drawer when pounding started at the door.

"Help us!" someone shouted.

Double fucksticks, Ree thought, hopping the desk and barreling for the door.

CHAPTER THREE

Repeat Customers

Ree deactivated the wards on the door locks as fast as she could, while the sounds of pounding, scratching, and shouting came through loud and clear.

"Boss, we've got trouble out here!" Ree shouted back across the room as she grabbed the door handle, her other hand on her lightsaber.

Ree threw open the door and thumbed on the weapon, the blue blade leaping to life as she tapped into the collective nostalgia for lightsabers' awesomeness, transforming the prop into a fully functional elegant weapon from a more civilized age.

She kept the blade behind her as customers came streaming in, pushing past her to escape . . . what?

Ree looked past everyone into the dark of the sewers. As she looked down to the concrete pathways at the side of the tunnels, she saw them: Gnomes. Lots of gnomes. There were dozens of the scrawny bearded things, tearing at Grognard's patrons with yellowed claws and jagged teeth. Several customers were pinned by the gnomes, so Ree jumped out into the tunnel and laid into the nasty little biters, chopping limbs and heads off while trying very hard to make sure none of her customers got the vorpal treatment.

I wonder if this will get me employee of the month? Or at least some hazard pay, she thought. As she Cuisinart™-ed her way through the crowd, pushing the creatures off of a bloodied Shade, she realized that there were too many to run off.

"Close the door as soon as I'm in, okay?" she yelled, hoping someone inside was holding on to their wits instead of their asses.

Ree cut a leaping gnome in half, then caught another one with a crescent kick. Bastards could jump, that was for sure. She stepped back toward the doorway, holding the lightsaber low to fend off the creatures.

"Shade, you hear me?" she asked, feeling the Cyberpunk behind her.

"Uhhn" was his response.

"Someone get Shade inside!" Ree said, spinning the blade and catching another pair of gnomes. There were too many. A third dodged away from her swings and took a swipe at her leg, its tiny claws tearing through her jeans like a set of X-acto knives. The pain dropped her to a knee.

She kept her sword up by sheer fucking determination fueled by her desire to not be eaten alive by creatures that shared a name with a beloved children's cartoon.

When she clocked out, it wasn't going to be to these things. She could accept a heroic final stand, saving the lives of dozens from unspeakable creatures or, preferably, a painless death at the age of ninety-something, surrounded by family and adoring fans. But not in a stinky-ass sewer, eaten alive by gnomes while making ten bucks an hour plus tips.

Ree reached into her apron and pulled out a *Magic: The Gathering* card, a *Circle of Protection: Black*. She guessed that the creatures would count as Black, being scavenger-y and half-dead-looking. She tore the card in half, hoping for a reprieve.

A small globe leapt up, pushing the creatures back. Ree whooped internally, taking the opportunity to flip her lightsaber off and grab Shade. She dragged the injured man along the concrete floor until she reached the edge of the circle. There were about two yards between the edge of her circle and the threshold of the store, and Shade was not a small man.

"Little help?" she asked.

Drake Winters strode through the door, his rifle flashing with bolts of green energy that ripped into the gnomes, covering her retreat.

"Did you ever know that you're my hero?" Ree said as she dragged Shade back inside.

The adventurer failed to respond to her song reference, though she doubted it had even registered. Ree and Drake got on smashingly, but when she went to the pop culture reference place with him, she might as well have been speaking Swahili. Unless she went Victorian or older—those he got.

But he didn't need to appreciate the joke to cover her ass, so Ree dropped Shade inside the store in front of frustratingly useless customers. Her second-best friend, adrenaline, helped her move on the injured leg, but it was going to hurt like the thousand-and-one Chinese hells when this was all done.

"That everyone?" Ree asked, moving up to Drake's side to scan the tunnel.

"It appears so."

Satisfied, Ree stepped back on her good leg and started pulling the door closed. This, at least, seemed safe enough for the other customers to help, save Wickham, who sat at the table like she was sipping a Piña Colada on the beach.

"So nice of you to help, Lieutenant," Ree said as the door settled closed. Ree activated all of the locks, then exhaled and slumped against the door.

"You appeared to have everything in hand. And it is not my responsibility as a customer to protect the other patrons."

Ree restrained an eye roll.

Drake crossed to the bar and leaned his rifle against a table.

"The welfare of other humans has never been the concern of the fair Lieutenant. Her concerns are greater, to hear her tell of it."

Wickham gave a nasty smile. "He can be taught. Or was that insight delivered to you by Providence, the same way you get everything else?"

Drake crossed his arms, leaning back into a defensive position. "And now you doubt even that I have insights of my own?"

Wickham threw her arms open. "Why not? Everything else just falls into place for you. Your jury-rigged contraptions make MacGyver look like a paragon of humanist engineering."

She pulled a small firearm off her belt. "This weapon shoots stunning darts using a pneumatic system. But unlike your geegaws, it works because of science. My friend Dr. Einsteinium spent seven months refining the design and testing it until it was safe."

Wickham waved dismissively at Drake's belt. "That Hellboy gun of yours? It's not scientifically possible. It flaunts the laws of physics like a tween god on a sugar bender, and you cobbled it together in, what, a weekend? You're a magician, Drake, nothing more. You can dress it up with technobabble, but at the end of the day, you're no more a scientist than Ree or the rest of them."

Drake's sharp intake cut across the silent room. Ree's vision went hot on his behalf.

The adventurer's voice shook, but he kept his tone level, his words measured. "How many worlds have you been to, Wickham? Based on what cross-dimensional scientific tradition and scientific analysis are you making such an unequivocal statement demeaning my work?"

"We're on Earth, the only world I care about. And here, your inventions are not science. Your crap is dragging Steampunk down from its progressive potential, prompting the masses to treat it as just another bit of fluff with impossible devices and pretentious names. Every time you use one of your artifacts, it undercuts the market for real science. Leave the movement to the actual scholars and actual, real engineers helping point a way forward by reclaiming a personal relationship to technology."

Ree looked to Drake. The corner of his lips had curled into a snarl, and he looked like he was holding an explosion in, refusing to come down to her level.

That's fine, Ree thought. She was more than happy to play in the gutter on his behalf. "Fuck off, Wickham. Who died and made you queen arbiter of what is and isn't Steampunk? K. W. Jeter is still around and kicking, and unless you're much older than you look and have been writing under a pseudonym, you don't have the right to tell anyone what they can or can't call Steampunk. Seriously, why don't you go home and circle-jerk your awesome friends and their artisanal bespoke hoojabs and leave Priya and Drake alone," Ree said, completely out of patience.

"Enough, children," Eastwood said, lit in profile by the lantern.

Where were you a second ago? Ree wondered.

There were a half-dozen customers in the bar now, including Shade. That left another eight or nine that hadn't come back or hadn't made it back.

"We only got two turns out when we saw them," said Chandra, a *Warhammer 40K* specialist with a red-and-blue Mohawk and vintage punk attire. She walked over to the table and picked up Uncle Joe's pint glass, taking a long swig before setting it down. Uncle Joe just shrugged as Chandra leaned against a chair, obviously pained.

"It's like they were waiting for us. Must have been fifty of them, falling over one another to attack. Juno was the first one out, they jumped her almost before we could move. We got back as soon as we could, but I was in the middle of the pack when we left, and . . ." Chandra turned, and Ree drew in a sharp breath through her teeth. The woman's outfit was shredded. Her jacket, skirt, and fishnets had gone from the intentionally ripped-up of punk to honest-to-Johnny-Ramone torn to tatters.

"Holy crap. How are you still standing?"

Chandra indicated her dozen facial piercings—nose, lip, ear, and eyebrow. "I've got more than a dozen piercings and as many tattoos. That, plus a few years in the fetish scene, adds up to a pretty righteous pain tolerance."

Ree pounded a fist against her chest. "Respect."

Grognard walked back to the bar, rummaged around, set something on the counter, and pulled out the bottle of Macallan 18.

He poured three fingers and then returned with the fishing box first-aid kit to hand the tumbler of whiskey to Chandra. "Sit."

Chandra sniffed the glass, cracked her neck, then took the drink all at once. She shook her head as she set the tumbler down, then lowered herself onto a chair with care.

Eastwood went to the door, Drake found himself a seat, and Ree rummaged through her apron for one of the healing potion tokens she'd started carrying. Grognard had his Cure Major Wounds Stout, but that one had 17.5% ABV, and the potion had nada.

Ree put the token in her teeth and twisted, tearing the cardboard. Warm energy hit her like a shower, and the pain in her leg vanished. She sighed, spitting the cardboard token into her hand and stretching the formerly injured foot.

"So, what now, boss?" Ree asked.

Grognard didn't look up from his kit. His medic box dwarfed Ree's magical sideboard, and between a couple of airplane bottles of Grognard's ale and some bandages, Chandra's wounds were downgraded from "Get thee to a hospital!" to "sleep it off" in a couple minutes flat.

When he was done, he looked up and addressed Ree's question. "Now we gear up and kick those miniature sons of bitches off of my front door."

Grognard turned to the group. "Load up, folks. If you didn't bring weapons"—he paused—"I suppose you can borrow something from my armory. But unless you want Ree to ring you up when this is done, *borrow* is all you get to do."

Most everyone nodded. Eastwood ignored him, checking his own weapons on an adjacent table. He had out his lightsaber, his Han Solo blaster, a bowie knife, his Green Lantern power ring, and several worn stacks of CCG cards held together with rubber bands. He'd be fine.

Uncle Joe, Talon, and the others made their way to the store section, bringing the lantern and their individual lights with them. Ree was reminded of the time her friendly local game store held a midnight party for the release of *D&D* 3rd edition and had turned the shop into their best imitation of a classic medieval tavern, serving root beer in steins and providing flashlights for browsing. Since going to Gen-Con and seeing True Dungeon's True Tavern, it had paled in comparison, but the preteen Ree had thought it was the shit.

Ree dumped the contents of her apron onto a table, checking what she'd actually brought with her and not just what she thought she'd tossed in. She'd been talking to her dad while getting ready for work, and he'd been cracking her up with stories of his last doomed date, this one with a life coach who had no degree and no experience, and as far as her dad could tell, just quoted *The Secret* to people. But hey, whatever works.

She had her lightsaber, a small CCG sideboard, two more healing potions (almost time to buy a new copy of *Descent*), a DS9-era phaser, and her most important tool, her phone. Rather than getting a separate iPod for media, Ree had just hollowed out the memory of games, apps, and music, and loaded it up with movies and film clips for an on-the-go Geekomantic grimoire.

So, what to watch? She probably wouldn't have time for a full movie or even a TV episode, so she loaded her playlist and started scrolling—she'd retitled the videos for easier power sorting.

ALPHAS—Superspeed—"The Quick and The Dead"

BUFFY—Bruiser suite—"Chosen"

SHERLOCK—Sherlock-vision—"A Study in Pink"

SPIDER-MAN—Whatever a Spider Can—Spider-Man and more.

Ree scrolled, pondered, then looked up. Several other customers were staring at their own phones and tablets.

"Let's coordinate. What are you all using for power boosts?" Not every Geekomancer could use genre emulation straight from the media—some, like Eastwood, had to destroy a physical object to get the power, the way that she used potions for healing.

"I've got *The Matrix*," said Chandra.

"*Conan the Conqueror*," said Talon as she hefted a longsword from the armory section of the store.

Ree looked around, but the others weren't volunteering.

"Thanks," Ree said, then went back to her pondering. Pearson's magical underground wasn't like the *Dresden Files*, where the magicians had a White Council, or Harry Potter, with the Ministry of Magic. In Ree's experience so far, it was more like being in a subcultural scene—you knew some people well enough to call friends, and everyone else was just kind of there. It was less pressure, but it meant that people weren't big on watching one another's back.

Out of the people there, Ree had fought alongside only Drake, Eastwood, and Talon. Uncle Joe would be all cards, all the time, tearing into his CCG collection for one-shot magic effects. That is, if he could bring himself to destroy any cards. This was, after all, the guy who would reorganize Grognard's card sleeves to be alphabetical by author and who sleeved cards as soon as he opened his booster packs.

As for Chandra, Ree didn't know what to expect. She didn't know how either the punk or Uncle Joe moved in combat, whether they communicated, how well they stood up under pressure. Nada.

Heading out into the sewer was going to have all the awkward of a first RPG session or a pickup group in an MMO—lots of chaos, no established rhythm or cohesion. If they were tripping over one another like newbs, the night was not going to end well. And where a TPK in a game would mean a lousy evening, a wipe here would be substantially more permanent.

Ree took a seat and hit play on her favorite clip from *Spider-Man*, hoping that the climbing and jumping would help her take the fight 3D—if she was standing upside down on the ceiling, she'd be less likely to trip over her fellow geeks.

When the clip was done, Grognard coughed and gathered people's attention. He stood by the door, wearing a chain shirt over a padded gambeson, as well as gauntlets and shining metal knee and elbow cops. Against his shoulder, he held a glaive-guisarme, one of the obscure polearms beloved by the late Gary Gygax, Godfather of *D&D*.

"Everyone ready?" he asked.

The chorus of clicks, chunks, rattles, and powering-up sounds continued for a moment before fading.

"Here's how we're going to do it," Grognard said. "My shop, my call. Everyone stay tight, and watch one another's backs. If they split us up, we're hosed. First priority is keeping them out of the shop. If they get in, we have no place to fall back to. If you see a gap through their numbers, you do not go alone. We all get out at once, or no one gets out. We have food and water here to last several days, even without power, so we can take them in waves. But the wards on the door won't last forever, not under that amount of pressure, so we have to clear the hall first."

This is not his first rodeo, Ree thought, as if the way he handled the weapon and moved in the armor left any doubt.

Most armchair generals and old-school miniature geeks didn't have practical experience in battle because really, in twenty-first-century America, most people didn't have combat experience, unless you were in gangland or live on a military base. But Grognard talked like a veteran sergeant or master chief.

"Got it?" he asked. Everyone nodded.

Note to self: Sometimes Strength or Will can replace Charisma for leadership checks. True story.

Grognard turned to Ree. "Keep an eye on everyone. What are you specced with?"

"Friendly Neighborhood Spider-Man," Ree said.

"Then you're on flanking duty. But don't stick around and try to hero it up if things get bad. I have no interest in training another employee anytime this decade, you hear me?"

Ree saluted with her lightsaber. "Aye aye."

Grognard grunted in approval. "Form up. Tall folk in the middle, melee folks in front. Area attacks first so we can clear some ground, then we take and hold it. Don't let them cut us off from the door, and for the love of Gygax, communicate out there."

Eastwood piped up. "The rutting little things can jump more than you give them credit for, so don't think you can keep on top of them. Some snort like bulls before they charge, so watch out for that, too."

Ree didn't bother looking at Eastwood. She'd learned all of that firsthand. But it was good advice, she had to give him that.

A quick head count told her something was off. Ree looked over her shoulder and saw that Wickham was still standing back in the store section, adjusting the straps on her outfit.

"Care to join us?" Ree asked, trying to bleed as much snippiness out of the statement as she could. It wasn't usually a great idea to antagonize people you're hoping will watch your back.

Wickham huffed, struggling with the straps. "I can't imagine what hapless jackanape made this abysmal excuse for a harness."

Ree shared a look with Grognard and walked back over to Wickham, her weapon down. "Here, let me. This was made by a lefty—that's why it's still on the shelf."

Wickham sighed in exasperation, tossing her pistol aside. Restraining another eye roll, Ree went to the ranty model to help her out.

"Hold still a minute." Wickham did, and for a moment, they were just two women, one helping another with a wardrobe malfunction.

Until Wickham opened her mouth again. "You're a poor excuse for a lady in waiting, but considering my options . . ." she said, gesturing to the rest of the group. Talon and Chandra were the only other women present.

"And you're a crap excuse for a noblewoman, so we go together just fine," Ree said, flipping a strap and releasing a clasp. The Spider-magic was fueling her natural tendency toward quippy retorts. Thankfully, she'd established that banter seemed to come free with the genre emulation. "There, that should do it."

Wickham straightened herself out of Ree's grasp and stretched, testing her range of motion. "That will have to do."

Ree crossed her arms. "You must have missed the 'please' and 'thank you' unit in kindergarten."

"I skipped kindergarten," Wickham said.

"I rest my case." Ree threw up her arms and went back to the door, her lightsaber out again. "Sorry," she said to Grognard.

"And what happened to 'Protecting the other patrons is not my responsibility'?" Ree asked in Wickham's direction.

The Lieutenant scoffed. "I realized that the only way out of here would be to make an opportunity myself. Try not to get in my way."

Wickham sauntered over to the group, owning the role of Cordelia for their motley Scooby Gang. Since Wickham was looking away, Ree allowed herself the most indulgent of eye rolls as she followed.

Grognard unlocked the door, then hauled it open with one swing. He dropped into guard with his glaive-guisarme, Ree activated her lightsaber, and the others powered up their various weapons.

"Here we go!" Ree said.

CHAPTER FOUR

Dysfunctional Raid Party

The mass of gnomes looked like a beehive. They were stacked on top of one another, falling and scrambling over one another to get to the group.

Uncle Joe raised several cards over his head, tore them with a whoop, and a wave of fire pushed forward, enveloping the gnomes. They screamed and scuttled backward, and the group stepped forward into the sewer. Eastwood tossed out a handful of industrial-grade glow sticks, which filled the tunnel with yellow light.

Ree did her best Steve Ditko Spidey-fingers, unleashing a net of webbing that pinned a handful of gnomes to the far wall. She jumped forward and swung up, the blue blade strobing across her vision. She caught two of the gnomes, but several more leapt out of the way. As soon as her blade swung past, more of the miniature monsters scuttled forward. Their nails clicked on the concrete floor with the strange familiarity of her golden retriever, Booster, trying to get purchase in the linoleum kitchen back at her dad's place.

She let loose another dose of webbing, then jumped and stuck to the ceiling, leaving her sword arm free to continue swinging.

Ree's spider-shtick attracted a dozen of the gnomes' attention as they tried to climb over one another to get to her. Even with their considerable ups, they fell short, putting them just in range of her lightsaber.

From her vantage point, she saw the rest of the group as they fought, each in their own style.

Out front, Grognard tore through the creatures, swinging the glaive-guisarme around as easily as a broom at closing time.

Talon covered Grognard's back, following his movements and keeping the gnomes from sneaking through legs and flanking the group as they formed a semicircle out from the door. She fought with practiced efficiency, the longsword always striking and blocking at once as her hands moved in concert, levering the pommel around for maximum precision.

On the other side of the group, Eastwood fought with lightsaber and blaster in perfect harmony, managing not to chop his hand off even as he wove and dove through the crowd at a breakneck pace. He was a jerk sometimes, but he'd earned his Badass bona fides years ago. Gnomes jumped at him by the dozen, like they'd all decided he was the most delicious dish on the menu.

Drake stood back, picking his targets quickly but deliberately, squeezing off shots that thinned the herd rushing at Eastwood.

Wickham hugged the side of the door, taking shots where she could. She wasn't comfortable in a fight, but she'd logged plenty of practice time somewhere—range or arcade—so her shots connected more often than not. Trouble was, her peashooter only seemed to stun the gnomes.

A musty wind hit her cheek, and Ree looked down to see that the gnomes clustered beneath her had started to get smart. Two gnomes held their hands together, boosting up the others. Ree wanted to know where they'd picked up cheerleading techniques, but that would have to wait. She flattened against the ceiling to avoid a tall gnome's swipe, which fell just inches short.

The magical energy from *Spider-Man* was waning, as she'd only gotten a quick dose of the film. Rather than spending the energy on another burst of webbing, she cut the arm off the next gnome that got a boost. The gnome crashed into its accomplices, which would scatter them for a bit. Ree pulled out her phaser and zapped a few more, then turned and dropped one that had managed to Xenomorph its way along the ceiling, just a few feet from Wickham's head.

The sizzling gnome fell to the sewer ledge in a heap at Wickham's feet, and the model looked up to Ree, who saluted.

"That's two you owe me," Ree said with a grin, then turned back to her cheerleader gnomes. She picked off the two boosters, hoping that they were the bearded brains of the operation. If Wickham responded, the sound was lost in the din. Gloating was hard to do when you were dead, so she could wait.

"How you feeling, boss?" Ree asked, her voice echoing in the sewer over the sound of clanging metal, exertion, and snarling.

"They don't seem to be running out of friends! Somebody pour on the AoE!" he called.

"On it!" Uncle Joe flipped through a card binder, then pulled out several cards, which he tore in half and then threw, Gambit-style. The card shreds flew true, exploding on impact. The blasts engulfed a dozen gnomes, but as the dust settled, more had filled the space, hopping over their charred compatriots.

"I didn't think there were that many in the whole city!" Ree said.

"Recent surveys put their numbers at under a hundred. We've seen at least twice that," Drake answered, his voice level even as his firing routine had become more harried. He stopped as one of the crystals in his aetheric rifle went dark, and cleared the gem, replacing it with a ruby red one that Ree knew as his flamethrower mode.

"Clear!" Drake called, and Talon cycled right, opening up a space. The inventor knelt forward and the rifle belched a cone of flame that took another cluster of the gnomes. The repeated blasts turned the sewer into a sauna, including the concrete she held on to with Spider Power. It was either burn her ass off or lose the higher ground, so she dropped from the ceiling, cleaving through several gnomes as she landed.

When she hit the concrete pathway near the group, the sewer shook.

"Someone needs to lay off the lagers," Wickham said.

"That wasn't her," Grognard said, looking down the tunnel.

A roar shook the walls of the sewer, making it very apparent that the gnomes were no longer the worst of their problems. If possible, the smell in the tunnel got worse.

That's never a good sign. In her nine months of hero-ing, she'd noticed a clear correlation between "smells bad" and "likes to snack on humans and suck the marrow from their bones nom nom nom" types of creatures.

"Boss?" Ree asked, closing ranks with Drake between one of the adventurer's bursts of flame. The gnomes on the roar side of the tunnel parted. *Even worse sign.*

Grognard buried the head of his blade in a gnome's shoulder, the butt of the haft held down with his foot. Then he used the weapon like a lever, slamming four gnomes into the wall with one heave. "Anyone got a land mine?" he asked.

"Let me check!" Uncle Joc said, flipping through his binder. "I just had a big order for a Direct Damage deck, haven't had a chance to restock."

A second roar gave way to the sound of charging and splashing sewage. The gnomes on the far side vanished into the shadows.

On one hand, it gave them a breather. On the other hand . . . "Faster would be better!" Ree said, quoting her favorite space cowboy.

Eastwood holstered his blaster and leveled his Green Lantern ring at the right side of the tunnel. Ree pointed her blaster in the same direction. The group formed their best imitation of a pike formation, reinforcing their position in the direction of the oncoming . . .

. . . Minotaur.

Really? Just what I fuckin' need.

The beast emerged from the shadows, lit by lightsaber and flare alike. It held an axe that made Grognard's polearm look like a toothpick.

"Fuuuuck," Ree said, and they all fired. Fire, laser, and lantern light hit the creature, but it kept coming, hunched over to fit its giganticness into the tunnel. The creature snorted out, and Ree realized that the thing wasn't going to stop.

Ree knelt to add her lightsaber to the pike formation. From over her shoulder, she saw another beam of green energy, and then the sewer was filled by a half-opaque green-colored brick wall.

"This won't work. Everyone back inside," Eastwood said.

The Minotaur hit the wall, and she saw the construct crack. Eastwood was sweating, his teeth gritted so tight, he was risking lockjaw.

Grognard stood, backing away. "You heard him. Everyone inside. We need bigger guns for this thing."

"The way is clear!" Wickham said, pointing left. We can go!"

Drake said, "It's a ruse. The gnomes will only be waiting for us around the next bend. This is the proverbial Scylla and Charybdis," he said as the Minotaur hammered away at Eastwood's wall.

The cowboy clasped his free hand around the other. His face was drenched with sweat.

"No time," Ree said, grabbing Wickham by the wrist and pulling her back and into the gap that opened when Grognard pulled on the door.

The group rushed inside, and Ree ducked back into the tunnel to haul a sweat-slicked Eastwood after them as his construct crumbled and dissolved.

The Minotaur's horn bounced off Grognard's wards on the door, but the hammering continued even as the brewmaster closed the last latch.

Two sounds echoed at once as the Minotaur hit: the *thud!* of impact and the *zot!* of Grognard's wards hitting the Minotaur back with the magical equivalent of a Mack truck. Ree wasn't sure which was actually harder.

Ree pushed herself off the door and hunched over, resting her hands on her knees. *Eat your heart out,* P90X. *Action Hero is the new extreme exercise system.* Guaranteed to keep off the pounds, just as long as your life stays consistently perilous.

The others collapsed to their knees or onto chairs. Eastwood splayed out on the ground, his chest heaving.

"Well, that could have gone better," Ree said between gasps. She stood up and went to the bar to draw a pitcher of water. The pitcher went on a tray, along with several glasses. Ree balanced the tray against her hip and brought the water back to the group. This was something she could control, a chance to do something useful and distract herself from the totally-not-ominous-please-make-it-stop pounding at the door.

Grognard took the mug with a nod, then poured glasses and handed them out. "The wards will hold. Not forever, but long enough to put together some heavier weaponry and take that thing out. With preparation and this arsenal"—he gestured to the room—"we should be able to take on pretty much anything."

Several heads nodded, muttering agreement. Eastwood just kept breathing. Ree had never tried to use a lantern power ring, but if their rules applied, it would be a herculean task to make and maintain a construct like he'd done. It just might have saved their lives.

Ree took a glass of water and went over to the scruffy man. She leaned over to get his attention.

"You okay?"

Eastwood lifted his head and opened bloodshot eyes, then set his head back down and lifted himself up to a sitting position. He took the water and chugged the whole thing in one go. When it was all done, he sighed and said, "Thanks. You?"

"Didn't get touched. That's a hell of a feat you just pulled off."

"Had to be done." He turned to the group. "Don't think I could do it again anytime soon, though."

Drake set his rifle down against the table. "Perhaps we should reexamine the office exit, then flank the creature."

"No. The wards work best when I'm in the shop," Grognard knocked on his chest. "Proximal resonance. We'll have to take it head-on. Joe, you're the artillery here. What can you do?"

Uncle Joe was wrapped tight around his binder, shaking. He didn't respond.

"Joe?" Grognard said.

"Nope. No. Not me. I'm no hero," he said.

Chandra knelt down next to Joe and put a hand on his shoulder.

"Joe, we're all in this. We all get out or no one gets out."

Joe was shaking, his hands wringing, eyes downcast. "I've already lost too much. I just spent five hundred dollars in singles, and for what? We're still screwed. We should just reinforce the door and wait until they give up."

Grognard shook his head. "Turtling might work in *V:TES*, but I'm not going to just sit on my ass and buff the door all night."

Wickham said, "If there's such an arsenal in here, why do we need to worry about the door? We hit it with everything when it comes inside, then we dust our hands off and walk away. It's not complicated, people."

"By all means, then, give us your plan, Lieutenant," Drake said. Ree could hear the hint of anger in his voice, though he hid it with all the skill of a nineteenth-century-esque gentleman. Ree still wasn't 100 percent sure whether his home world was an alternate Earth, a parallel Earth, a subcreated Earth, or just an Earth specifically designed to be confusing.

Wickham crossed her arms, striking a cover-ready pose as she thought. "It shouldn't be hard to create a field of cross fire, then lay down wards to channel it into a kill zone."

"Why even let it inside? Can't we put the wards on the threshold, open the door, and take pot shots from in here?" Ree asked.

"We could," Drake said, walking back into the group. His head was bandaged up, making an odd sight with his goggles over a covered eye. "But the ward lines will disrupt any magical offensive, even with monodirectional wards."

"So what will work?" Ree asked. "It's not like we don't have options," she said, gesturing to the store side of the room.

"I'm not letting those things in my store, Ree. Discussion over," Grognard said.

Talon continued, "Anything associated with Theseus will give us a boost, or barring that, something Greek will work a bit better than normal." She went to the sword wall and pulled down a simple one-handed sword. "This Greek or Babylonian?"

Grognard shook his head. "Phoenician. Don't have any Greek in stock."

"I have a whole Greek kit set up . . . in my shop," she said, setting the sword back on its hanger.

Talon said her magic was still Geekomancy, but from where Ree stood, it was a whole different animal. Where Ree connected with characters for superpowers or skills with her magic, across her full range of fandom, Talon's Geekomancy drew directly on the fighting styles and weapons. If Ree was a Geekomantic Bard, Talon was All-Fighter, All-The-Time. Talon could match weapons and the armor to a movie or show to min-max her way to godly Fighter status. But she was more than dangerous enough with any weapon that she could tie to a film.

"So, barring that, just heavy-duty magic," Ree said, trying to keep the conversation rolling in the get-shit-done direction, since the pounding on the door wasn't letting up, though she noted that the *zot* sounds were a lot softer and the gaps between *thud*s shorter.

"The combined efforts of a half-dozen blasts and blows rolled off of that creature like it was an afternoon drizzle.

Merely repeating our previous folly stands little chance of success. We must think smarter, not bigger," Drake said, adjusting a gauge on his rifle.

"So why are you talking?" Wickham said.

Something inside Ree snapped. *That's it.*

"You know what? Fuck you, you worthless piece of shit. You belittle my friends, you can't be bothered to pick a real weapon for a fight, and you've got your head stuck so far up your own ass that you can use your boobs for goggles."

Wickham's head snapped back like she'd been slapped. Another minute, and Ree might just do that anyway. *Fuck with me is one thing. Fuck with my people and you can bleed out in a cold alley right in front of me while I keep sipping my cappuccino.*

Ree had raised the rage stakes, and now Wickham was calling. "You arrogant, foul-mouthed cretin! I could have left you all in the dust during that fight, but no! I was a team player. I may not be a nerd, but I got in there and did my part. If that's not enough for you, that's not my problem. But if you insist on shooting down every single one of my ideas . . ." Wickham tore at the harness, struggling and twisting in place.

She abandoned the effort and continued her rant. "Ideas that will actually solve the problem instead of just creating more chances for your merry band of pathetic losers and shut-ins to try to capture a sliver of the hope of echoing the glory of impossible-bodied heroes from facile excuses for literature and film!"

Ree let the ridiculous offensiveness of the statement roll over her, then cracked her head to the side. No one else was interjecting, and Ree was perfectly happy to take on this fight herself.

"I get that you're afraid of getting your designer gear even the tiniest bit dirty while the rest of us do the hero-ing, but why do you even come here, if you think so little of us? Grognard's booze is great, but if you have to soil your designer faux-vintage frock just sitting on the bar stool, why not grace more refined establishments with your beatificness?"

Ree took another step toward Wickham. "Or maybe you've gotten your finely toned condescending ass kicked out of all of the ritzy places, and this is the closest you can get to a scene bar? Worst of all, do you just come to mock us, to sip your scotch and laugh at all the freaks? Please tell me there's more to you than tearing people down, because right now, all I see is everything that's wrong with entitled high-culture bougieness."

Wickham stepped forward like she was going to escalate, but she didn't raise a hand. She got up into Ree's face, and said in a slow, measured, but obviously furious tone, "I don't have to justify myself to you, you self-righteous, infantile fangirl. Instead of hard work, you have DVD boxed sets. Instead of making your own artifacts, you buy them off of eBay. Everything special about you was made by someone else."

Against all odds, Ree managed to pass her Willpower check and did not lay Wickham out on the floor with a punch. Instead, the two women stared at each other with dagger eyes.

An interminable moment later, Grognard interposed himself between the women, his powerful frame forcing them apart.

"Cut it out. We have bigger fish to fry. Wickham, if you think that little of my shop and my patrons, you can consider yourself un-invited. Don't ever set foot in here again, effective as soon as we get ourselves out of this situation."

Wickham backed off a step, turning her back on Ree.

Ree cracked her back, then turned to face the group. She let the rage seep out in one long breath. "So. Firepower." She walked to the collected geeks licking their wounds. "I'm guessing piercing weapons will be best. Maybe we can pin the thing into the sewer if we stick it enough times. The bugger is almost too big for the tunnel in the first place."

Talon picked up on Ree's thread. "We can make a cross-hatch of weapons, do the pike square right. Add that to some piercing ranged weapons, maybe a few explosions . . ."

Eastwood shook his head. "Still won't be enough. I'll bet the Dorkcave that it has a supernatural resistance. If we don't find the thing's vulnerability, it won't matter how much abuse we heap on the thing. Before anything else, we need a Detect Weakness effect."

"On it." Ree went to the comic aisle, her mind already giving her a solution. She ran her fingers over the place cards until she reached *F*, then started scanning issues of *Fantastic Four*. The Inhumans character Karnak could find the weakness in any person, object, or plan—just what the doctor ordered. His oddly precise power meant he was never a major-league threat, but he made an excellent secondary foil or, in this case, the ally who offered the key to the puzzle.

She flipped back to some of the earliest *Fantastic Four* comics, since using a first appearance would give her the biggest dose of the character's power. She might be able to use the *Ultimate*-verse version or a recent issue, but if the creature had magical protections, she might need to overcome that protection even when it came to finding a weakness.

The folks at the bar kept chatting while Ree flipped through bagged and boarded comics—#48, #47, #46 . . .

"Here!" Ree said, pulling out a comic that proclaimed AMONG US HIDE THE INHUMANS! in typical Stan Lee/Jack Kirby bombasticity. This was the only copy on hand, and if Ree's suspicion about needing its primacy was right, they'd get only one shot.

Ree brought the comic over to the group. "So here's the next question. Do we try to hedge our bets and pick a variety of things we think could work, then try to use one as soon as Karnak here helps us out, or do we risk a quick peek just to do the scouting on horny and persistent out there?"

The group considered. Chin in hand like a standing Thinker, Drake tapped his cheek with a finger, then said, "It would be unwise to trust that we will be both wise enough and fortunate enough to have preselected the right solution. I believe we should separate the two steps."

Eastwood shook his head, arms crossed. "There's no guarantee we can contain that thing even once more. When that door opens, we have to leave abso-frakking-lutely everything on the table."

Chandra clicked her tongue ring against her teeth, pondering.

Uncle Joe calmed his shaking for a moment, saying, "We can't let that thing in here. No way." Joe looked like the movie version of shell-shocked. Ree didn't know if she'd ever seen PTSD firsthand in an identifiable way; it's not like people wore hats advertising their mental health challenges. But one way or another, she wasn't betting on him making it through another skirmish.

Wickham had adjourned to the bar. Beside her sat a bottle of Johnnie Walker Blue, two hundred-dollar bills out next to it. Whatever else Ree could say about Wickham, the woman wasn't a thief.

"We have to split it up," Grognard said. Ree looked back to the group, leaving Wickham to her top-shelf moping.

The barkeep continued, "There are too many possibilities. We can't guarantee we'll be ready with the solution. I'll open the door, and I want Talon and Eastwood with me to hold it off. Ree, you use the comic and get the intel. When you've got it, tell us and we close the door. Then we make the rest of the plan. All right?"

The group nodded. Talon swapped her longsword out for a naginata, and Eastwood added a blue lantern ring next to his green.

"I don't know whether to hate Geoff Johns or call him a genius," Ree said, gesturing to the rings.

Eastwood shrugged. "It works. *Darkest Night*'s the best thing DC's done in years."

"I was always more of a Jack Kirby cosmic girl," Ree said.

The other geeks gathered themselves up, each preparing in their own eccentric ways. Uncle Joe wobbled to his feet, muttering under his breath as he rearranged several cards into the first page of sleeves. Chandra hauled a shield approximately the size of Grognard across the room. Ree met the punk halfway, and they walked the *scutum* together, leaving it against the interior wall next to the door. Shade was still out for the count. Grognard had produced a blanket from somewhere and had it draped over the unconscious techie. Drake attached a bayonet to the end of his rifle, and had a black crystal loaded in the chamber.

"I don't think I've ever seen that one. Do I want to know what it does?" she asked as the group made themselves ready by the door.

"No," said Drake and Grognard, in chorus.

"Roger that," Ree said. She had her lightsaber strapped to her belt, phaser tucked into her apron, and had retrieved the issue of *Fantastic Four* #45, removing it from its case. It'd been a while since she handled a comic this old with her bare hands. As an undergrad she'd held an *Amazing Fantasy* #1 at the Rollins Rare Books Library, but that was with gloves. Now even touching the issue gave her a charge.

Ree flashed back to something Eastwood had told her, about a friend of his tearing up an *Action Comics* #1 to fight off a tornado, and lost herself for a moment in the fantasy of how prepostrously cool that would be.

The sound of splintering brought her back to reality. The *zot!* of Grognard's wards had vanished completely.

"That's our cue," Grognard said, releasing the locks in record time.

"Have fun!" Wickham said from the bar, waving with her middle finger. Ree's ears burned, but she didn't have time to be snippy back.

The brewmaster counted in a hurried voice, "One."

Ree held the comic over her head, in both hands. *I didn't even get to read it,* she realized. She'd probably read the issue some time in the past, but never the original glossy, with its faded colors and smell of history.

"Two." Drake exhaled, his rifle held vertically beside Grognard, Eastwood at his side.

"Three."

CHAPTER FIVE

Karnak Knows Best

All at once, Grognard threw open the door, Eastwood tossed a fresh flare into the darkness, Talon and Chandra set the road-block-pike formation, and Ree tore the comic.

A flash of magic washed up her hands, arms, and then to her eyes.

The Minotaur loomed large in her vision, its fur burnt and horns partially melted by Grognard's wards. But it kept coming, rushing forward at the opened door.

And as it moved, Ree saw the Minotaur in a combination of a first-person shooter HUD and a Terminator's threat assessment screen. Circles popped up over the Minotaur's horns, hide, axe, and the ring through its nose.

Minotaur—*Huge Size*

Axe—*Huge*

Hide—*Hardened against magic, piercing, slashing, and bludgeoning*

Horns—*Deals damage to magical wards*

Nose ring—*Vulnerable only to grappling. If removed, will remove magical protection on hide.*

"Got it!" Ree shouted.

The Minotaur dove forward, leading with its horns, trying to force its way inside the door while Grognard and the others pulled on the heavy iron ring to close the door again.

"Watch out!" Ree shouted as the horn broke the threshold of the door, catching Eastwood across the right shoulder. The older geek snarled in pain, but held on with his left arm. The Minotaur got its head inside the door. From there, Ree knew it could pull the door open and then they'd all be hosed. She reached down and grabbed at the nose ring.

"Grab the ring!" she shouted, hauling on the metallic ring with all her might. Sadly, that wasn't much. The ring didn't budge, didn't even seem to get the creature's attention.

The world moved in slow-mo around her as Drake fired into the creature's face, Talon and Grognard hacked at its nose, and the door started to wrench open.

"Help!" Ree shouted as the Minotaur shook its head, worming its way inside. She ducked under the mangled horns, trying to keep her grip.

She kept hauling on the ring, pushing against the creature's snout with one foot. *Nothing doing.*

Another pair of hands joined hers on the ring—large, gnarled, bloodied: Grognard's. The pair of them pulled, but still it didn't budge.

"Get this thing out of my bar!" Grognard shouted. The Minotaur had the door half-open, and Ree saw the axe glimmering in the light of the flares. As she felt rank-smelling Huge-Axe-Decapitation-Doom growing undeniably closer, she composed a letter in her brain.

Dear Dad,

If you're reading this, then somehow my telepathic last

message has been imprinted on something and reached you in Indianapolis.

Turns out that when I said, "It's a bartending job, it's not going to kill me," I was a dirty liar. I've been hacked, dismembered, or otherwise murderated by a huge Minotaur alongside several of my closest secret-life friends and a snotty brat of a model (don't mind her).

Tell the Rhyming Ladies I love them, and I'm sorry.

And mostly, I have to say I'm sorry to you, because I've been holding out.

Love,

Your Departed Daughter

P.S. Morbid much?

Ree shook off the fatalism and snapped back to reality, where Eastwood was blasting away at the Minotaur with both power rings, blue and green beams hitting side by side.

And doing not a bloody thing.

"I've got it!" Uncle Joe said, and Ree heard the sound of tearing mixed with the release of magic.

A spectral hand popped into existence in front of the Minotaur. It swept Ree and Grognard off of the creature's snout, pushing them back into the bar.

"The fuck!" Ree said. But then, the hand pushed at the Minotaur, the hand larger than the creature's head. The Minotaur strained against the hand, snorting. Its eyes were red, and it had dropped the axe, pulling at the sides of the doorway. But inch by inch, the hand pushed the creature out of the door. Grognard leapt up and pulled the door shut, re-sealing the wards. "That door isn't going to keep it out for long," Ree said, looking back at Uncle Joe, who she suspected had pulled out the save.

"Was that a Bigby's Hand spell?" she asked.

Joe had crumpled to the floor, binder at his feet. "Mint Limited edition, from the canceled *Dungeons & Dragons* trading card spell expansion in 1992. They only made four test sheets. That was all of them."

Uncle Joe looked lost, hollowed out. Ree couldn't imagine how hard that must have been for him—giving up singular artifacts like that. That'd be like Ree burning the only remaining *Star Wars* laserdiscs, or the original scripts for *X-Men* #1. There were times when Geekomancy totally blew. In fifty years, would any of their material culture be left? *Or will people like me use it all up?*

She looked to the floor at the torn comic. Digital editions were replacing every medium in narrative—she'd heard some chatter about digital transition for Geekomancy, but every answer she heard raised more questions. Not to mention how it'd change the experience for readers and viewers.

Ree felt a hand on her shoulder, and she pulled herself out of the maudlin of self-reflection. It was Drake.

"Are you quite all right, Ree?"

Ree exhaled. "Yeah. I just wish we didn't have to destroy things for this magic."

"You don't have to," Drake said. "The more prepared you are, the more you can use the renewable sources. But these are pressing times, and your life is worth more than an individual incarnation of a text or a trading card."

Ree squeezed Drake's hand. *Why do you have to be dating Priya?* Ree whined to herself, then sighed and looked around the room, jumping back into the moment.

Across the bar, Wickham's movements were a shade sloppier, her bottle an inch emptier. The woman was actively ignoring the group. *Better than heckling,* Ree thought. Grognard stood by the door, rolling red-on-black dice while holding his back to the door. Eastwood was beside him, lending his middling weight.

"What's the word on the wards?" Ree asked.

Grognard cursed under his breath. "Shitty, that's the word. I can't reset anything while Toro out there is ripping my door to shreds."

"What can we do to help?" Chandra asked.

The brewmaster chuffed with his half-laugh. "Hold the door and pray to whoever you can get to listen."

The gang piled on to the door, which led to a reverse game of whack-a-mole, where they tried to keep away from the parts of the door being torn up by the Minotaur's horns. The door was quickly approaching the consistency of Swiss cheese, and shortly after that, it'd just shatter entirely.

"Wait. I can help." Uncle Joe flipped through his binder, and pulled out several square-edged cards. They looked hand-cut rather than machined like most CCG cards.

He joined the group, then tore up a card and put his hand to the door. Several of the gaps closed up.

"But first . . ." Uncle Joe tore up another card, then reached through one of the holes and slapped the cards on the opposite side.

A moment later, there was a *KABOOM!* from the sewer.

Uncle Joe grinned. "Explosive Runes."

"That thing can read?" Ree asked.

The cardmaster shrugged. Uncle Joe tore up another card, which closed the remaining gaps in the door.

"That should give you some time," Joe said.

Well, hot damn, Ree thought. "What's gotten into you?" she asked.

A wild smile hit Uncle Joe's face: the smile of a berserker or a wild scientist at the end of their rope. It was the face of "I no longer give a fuck."

"I've already dropped a grand tonight. What's another few hundred dollars?" he said.

Grognard rolled the dice once more, then whooped. There was another *thud,* but this time, it was met by an equally loud *zot.*

The brewmaster stood and slid the dice back into his apron. "That will hold it for a while. Now, how exactly do we kill that thing? The nose ring?"

Ree nodded. "If you pull the ring out of its nose, the immunity goes away. But it has to be done by hand. And it isn't exactly easy."

"So we need some superstrength," Eastwood said, stomping his way over to the store section.

"I got it," Ree said, producing her phone. She had clips to spare for this one. Namely, the entirety of "Chosen," since she found herself defaulting to Buffy powers so often.

"No good. We want superstrength multiplied by normal strength. It should be me," Grognard said. "Bring me those Hulk gloves."

Ree stepped up to the store section, then heard movement off to her right. She looked back to the group, then to a clearly inebriated Wickham at the bar.

"What was that?" she asked. *Mice? Cockroaches?* But it hadn't sounded like skittering. It was more like shuffling.

She stepped over an aisle and caught another flash of movement at the end of the row. "Ha!" she said, rushing down the aisle. Minotaur or no, she was not going to let some vermin run around and trash her (well, Grognard's) store.

"What the hell are you doing?" Grognard asked from across the room.

"There's something here, boss." Ree peeked around the corner of an aisle, and saw it.

The fuck? It was a *Warhammer 40K* Ork bike, painted red (naturally), from one of the pre-painted sets Grognard sold on commission.

And then, from behind her, she heard blaster fire. She hit the deck, turned, and saw that an Amidala's blaster pistol prop was firing at random, twitching on its rack.

"Boss, we've got a problem!"

All at once, the store went wild. Weapons fired off,

CCG cards jumped out of their sleeves, burst into flame, and then were replaced by summoned creatures, artifacts, and spell effects.

Great, I've gone from Assault on Precinct 13 *to* Jumanji, Ree thought, reaching for her lightsaber.

She commando-crawled her way to a corner, out of the lines of fire from the blasters, bow-casters, and the rest of Grognard's ranged armory. Unfortunately, that put her clear on the opposite side of the room from everyone else.

Drake and Grognard had taken cover behind an overturned table, firing at slivers, skeletons, oni, and other creatures that had appeared out of nowhere, summoned by Geekomantic artifacts gone haywire. Wickham had jumped the bar and was hiding, only the top of her hairpin visible over the bar rail.

Ree flashed her lightsaber on, hoping it had enough juice left in its nostalgia battery to get them through whatever wild magic was causing the store to go haywire.

She cut her way through a goblin from *Legend of the Five Rings*, then took the legs off of a robot from *Robo Rally*. She crawled on and found herself face-to-navel with a Troll Hunter from *World of Warcraft*. The Troll raised a rifle to shoot, and Ree dove forward, hacking at the creature as she went.

The Troll matched her acrobatics and backflipped up onto a table. It kicked several game boxes off of their perch, and as they crashed to the floor, the boxes burst open, pieces coming to life, a cluster of miniature space fighters from *Twilight Imperium* forming up and taking a strafing run at the Troll.

The Troll fired its rifle in her direction, taking a chunk out of the concrete floor. Ree slashed up at the table, forcing the Troll back.

More of the *Twilight Imperium* spaceships had taken flight, red and blue plastic figures warring with one another while the green pieces opened fire on the Troll. The Troll swatted the pieces out of the air, then did a round-off from the table. It drew a flaming blue machete and growled in her direction.

Behind her, a Maine Coon–size Mi-go took wing with a "Skree!" Ree caught a quick glimpse of the others as she looked back toward the Troll. Still pinned down by errant weapon fire, as well as a rampaging ogre with a tetsubo.

She saw the Troll just in time to jump aside to avoid its machete. The creature cartwheeled forward with its cut and Ree caught a kick to the head. She staggered backward and lashed out with the lightsaber, and when she opened her eyes again, the creature was missing a leg. She pressed the advantage and finished the Troll off with a thrust, then took up its machete in her left hand, preparing for the inevitable failure of her magic sword.

The Mi-go *skree!*-ed its way around the room, leaving Ree with an opening to get to the end of the aisle. From there, it was a straight shot to the bar, and to backup.

Behind her, the Troll popped into ichor like monsters do . . . but so did her machete. Ree dropped the goopified sword as fast as she could, but it still got a healthy splash of ichor on her pants.

At least these are work pants, Ree thought. She'd stopped wearing her good jeans to Grognard's when she and Drake got stuck in the sewer after Midnight Market.

Ree clicked off her lightsaber and switched out to the phaser as she did her best roadie-run along the aisle. Thirty feet . . . twenty-five.

And then Grey Dragon from *Alley Assault* jumped into the aisle and squared off against her, gray gi looking almost black in the low light. *Alley Assault* had never been more than an off-brand *Street Fighter*, but the pizza place Ree's dad had taken her when she was seven only ever had *Alley Assault*, and so she had a warm spot in her heart for the long-dead fighting franchise.

Ree opened fire, but Grey Dragon raised his hands and blocked, the energy dissipating against his muscled arms.

Balls. "It's going to be like that, is it?" Ree asked, taking a fighting stance. Dragon punched forward with one fist, shouting "Fireball!" A shimmering ball of silver-white energy leapt out at her, and she jumped over it, landing with a punch in Grey Dragon's direction, which he also blocked.

Ree fell into a crouch, and tried to sweep the leg in her best homage to the No More Kings song. But Grey Dragon shouted "Ascending Punch!" leaping into his uppercut and jumping over her kick.

But her years as an arcade rat had taught her the weakness of the Ascending Punch: if it missed, you were a chump the whole way down. Ree stood and reached out to grab Grey Dragon's gi, then slammed him to the ground with all her weight, which wasn't much.

But the throw got him out of her way, which is all she needed. She gamed the *Alley Assault* system, curb-stomping Grey Dragon in the head while he was on the ground, hoping it'd put him out. Not bothering to stop and see if it had, she booked it to the bar, power sliding under the legs of an ogre.

"Hi, guys. Did you miss me?" She leaned to the side as the ogre lashed out with the tetsubo again, biting into Grognard's sturdy-as-hell tables.

"Are these warded too?" she asked, pointing at the tables.

"Reinforced against everything under the magical sun. Especially stains," Grognard said.

"So why aren't these on the door?" Ree asked as she popped out from the table and fired her phaser at the ogre. It lurched back with the blow, giving Eastwood the chance to pour on fire from his blaster as well.

"Same wards. These just stay fresher." Grognard unscrewed a leg of the table and pulled out a plastic tube the size of Ree's forearm. It had a stash of cards, a few bandages, and a tiny bottle. Grognard popped the bottle cap off and downed the drink.

Then with a bellow, Grognard jumped over the table and delivered a thundering punch to the creature's midsection. It crumpled up, so the brewmaster laid the creature out with a right cross.

Ree looked to the other geeks behind the tables. "What was that?"

"That was my real Critical Hit ale," Grognard said. "The magic version takes twenty times as long to brew."

The ogre popped into ichor, causing a temporary lull in the bar section. But the elevated floor was still a madhouse. Several scenes played out, creatures and artifacts fighting among themselves. But at any moment, something else could decide to go for a new target.

Ree used the breather to pull out her phone for a quick power-up.

"Cover me?" she asked Drake.

"But of course," he said, keeping watch while he checked his ammunition stores.

Ree tapped her way through her playlist as fast as possible, replaying the scene from *Spider-Man* so she could change the game.

As she homed in on the scene, she heard the others chattering around her.

Chandra asked, "Does anyone know what's causing this ridiculousness?"

"Frak no," Eastwood said. "But I stopped wondering about stuff like this a long time ago."

"I've found that this city is very nearly as odd and prone to bizarre occurrences as the Deepness of Faerie," Drake said.

"You can say that again," Eastwood said. "But don't."

Drake chuckled. "That idiom I am familiar with, at least."

"There's hope for you yet, kid," Eastwood said.

"You're all nincompoops!" Wickham said, from behind the bar, her voice starting to slur.

Ree tried to shut out their banter and focus on the scene through the roaring, clanging, chattering, but it just wasn't happening.

She took a long breath, and restarted the clip. This time, she managed to keep the sounds out better, until a paper crane winged its way across her vision, then looped into a half-Immelmann over Eastwood and dive-bombed his face.

Eastwood reached out and caught the crane, which unfolded in his hand and started talking. It spoke in the voice of Lucretia d'Fete, one of the Pearson Underground. She was an Elegant Gothic Lolita Fate Witch, and was in no way a fan of Eastwood's.

Dear Anthony,

By now you will have had the fortune of enjoying the first phases of my vengeance for your despicable affront and robbery last fall. As revenge is a dish best served cold, I decided to inflict my fury on all those who would associate with you, including that nursemaid Grognard, with his childish clubhouse; your erstwhile upstart apprentice; and, well, whomever else happens to be around.

I thought it most appropriate to turn your little ritual tools against you. Perhaps robbed of your crutches, we will see what you're truly made of.

I look forward to gazing down on your bloodied broken corpse and reclaiming that which was stolen from me. And then I will leave you out in the street as a message to all in Pearson that to cross Lucretia d'Fete is to invite death and ruin.

With coldest regard,

Lady Lucretia d'Fete

Eastwood let out a string of what Ree assumed was cursing in either Mandarin or Cantonese. Ree suspected he'd repeated one of the longer curses from *Firefly*—"Holy Mother of God and all her whacky nephews" or "Shove all the planets of the universe up my ass"—Ree had learned some of the translations but not the curses themselves.

Grognard shook his head, cracking his knuckles. "When I

get my hands on that snooty, sanctimonious—"

The brewmaster's rage was cut short by a flurry of motion. Ree ducked back behind the table when she saw it coming, so the arrow that had been heading for her face managed to cut off only a chunk of her hair, making a gash through her cheek along the way.

"Cockwaffle!" she shouted as her hand went to her face. The cut wasn't deep, but if she hadn't moved, she would have become the punch line of a *Homestar Runner* joke.

Ree bent over and grabbed the small medical kit from Grognard's stash. Drake rolled between tables with his usual efficiency and set his rifle down at her feet.

"Why don't you let me do that," he said with a knowing smile.

Ree tried to focus on the fact that it was inadvisable to do first aid on your own face rather than the fact that it was a chance to have his hands on her face. *Yep. Staying good, that's me.*

Eastwood kept up the suppressing fire and Talon slashed at anything that got close enough to grab Ree's and Drake's cover. Grognard hadn't come back behind the cover.

"What the hell is Grognard doing?"

Drake peeked out from behind the table. "He appears to be wrestling a set of floating longbows."

Ree laughed, then instantly regretted it as moving her cheek opened the cut up even more.

"Please stay still," Drake said, only a hint of exasperation creeping into his voice.

She wanted to make another snappy comeback, but instead she took a long breath and let Drake apply the butterfly bandage. *But will I get a rad scar?* Ree wondered. *I probably don't want a rad scar. Unless I can get one on each cheek like Inigo Montoya.*

"There. That should suffice until we are able to get out of this morass," Drake said, taking up his rifle again.

"Thanks." Ree raised her phaser, and they nodded to each other. Ree looked around the table back into the fray, then took a pot shot at an orc that was waddling its way over with an oversized mallet.

The orc took her shot in the belly, and kept coming. Ree adjusted her fire upward, and her blast hit the thing in the head at the same time as Drake's green blast. The orc went down, and Ree changed targets.

If this was all Lucretia's doing, then it'd have to be chaos-oriented—her magic was all about fate, luck, destiny, and curses. The big question left was just how long the magic would hold out. It would take a huge amount of power to make Grognard's store go wild, but Lucretia'd had several months to weave the curse, in all likelihood. Ritual wasn't Ree's thing, but it seemed like with enough time, you could do nearly anything.

"Anyone have any bright ideas how to stop this curse?" Ree asked at a shout to be heard over the din.

Chandra spoke up. "High-grade counterspell ought to do it, but none of us are Hexomancers, so it'll be tricky no matter what."

A fighting robot flipped forward into the bar, energy staff spinning.

"Dibs," Eastwood said, jumping forward and igniting his lightsaber. The robot spun and slashed so fast, Ree could barely follow the motion. The two went blow for blow for a few seconds, but Eastwood's eagerness crumbled very quickly as he was forced to backpedal, gaining space to have the time to block the construct's strikes.

Ree fired off a shot with her phaser, but the killer robot blocked it, redirecting her continuous beam at Eastwood, who ducked and blocked with his own lightsaber, deflecting the beam into the ceiling, where it started to cut through the concrete. Ree cut off the beam and took up her own lightsaber.

However, taking the robot on was not going to be as easy or flashy as a two-on-one usually indicated. Neither Ree nor Eastwood had the Force guiding their blows, except in the general spiritual sense. *Though, maybe . . .*

Ree stepped forward with an upward cut, which the robot parried, responding with the other end of its staff. Ree ducked under the blow and sidestepped, trying to put the bad guy between the two of them without putting her back to the rest of the store. Which was pretty much impossible. But the robot was likely to kill her now, so she decided to focus on that. With the thing's attention split, Eastwood went back on the attack.

As the speed of the fight ramped up, faster and faster, Ree let years of martial arts training and lightsaber fights in the park take over, parrying, riposting, dodging, and pressing on instinct. Ree watched the fight almost from the outside, as if she were living a first-person fighting game. And it was awesome.

Even a short lifetime of martial arts training wasn't perfect, though, and Ree took a slash across her left arm from the robot as its torso spun around like a top, then pressed her.

Her sword in one hand, Ree backed up, trying desperately to ward off a hurricane of deadly light.

She found an opening in the robot's attack pattern, so she dove forward through the gap and stabbed at its torso. The construct turned aside at the last minute, but her blade still punched through the metal close to the arm hinge.

As Ree followed through with the roll, she heard another sound of lightsaber cutting through steel, and when she recovered, the killer robot's head toppled to the ground. Its staff flickered off, and the machine's torso collapsed beside the head.

Eastwood offered a hand, but Ree stood on her own.

The upside to lightsaber wounds, if there was such a thing, was that they were instantly cauterized (unless you were an Aqualish like Ponda Baba, apparently). But her forearm still felt like it had been doused in kerosene and then tossed into a bonfire.

Looking around, the store had become even more of a disaster zone, though the chaos was mostly feeding on itself, with only occasional attacks making their way over to the bar. But at this rate, there wouldn't be a single piece of merch left in salable condition. The store would be ruined, all so that Lucretia could have her stab at revenge on Eastwood for stealing back something that rightly belonged to him. *Fuckin' A.*

Grognard had taken a spot at the bar three seats down from a wobbly Wickham. He took a long draw from a bottle of his Adamantium Ale. The bottled versions of his brews were the real stuff, the ones with the magic. He served them sparingly, since the only thing worse than a mopey drunk magician was a mopey drunk magician with extra power.

"Are we going to stop this thing, or just wait until everything's broken?" Ree asked, trying to rally the troops, herself included.

"Gimme a minute. Not all of us are young like you or have a death wish like Eastwood." Grognard took a long swig from the bottle.

In chorus, Ree said, "Thanks," while Eastwood said, "Hey!" The bartender sighed and walked his way back over.

"Any new ideas?" Ree asked.

"Some of these things will just run down their nostalgia batteries. It'd take an epic amount of energy to keep them running past that point, and if Lucretia had that much power at her disposal, she'd probably just make Eastwood's heart explode."

The former astral cowboy squinted. "Seems like."

Drake stood from behind a table, his rifle still braced and ready. "If we could retrieve a few of the objects from the store, I believe I could concoct a countermeasure, absorb the ambient chaos energy, and convert it into another form. The project I've been working on was designed to answer a similar, if not identical, question. And I just so happened to have brought it with me today. It's in the back."

"How convenient!" Wickham said, slurring her words.

"Providence, my disbelieving . . . colleague." Ree chuckled to herself, as Drake clearly had to search for a moment to find a word that fit both his distaste and his manners. Drake had the uncanny knack to be where he needed to be when he needed to be there. And if it extended to knowing what tool to bring, Ree wasn't going to question him. The chances that Drake was collaborating with Lucretia were about one in a flobbidy-jillion.

"It's a deal. Get in there and start adjusting while things are at a lull," Grognard said, pointing his thumb back at the office.

Drake nodded and made for the office. Ree turned back to the storefront just in time to see an insectoid monster jump the railing.

"Shit!" Ree said, drawing her lightsaber in a hurry.

CHAPTER SIX

Speak Technobabble to Me, Baby

Talon lunged forward and stabbed at the mega-bug, intercepting it before it could pounce on Ree. The totally-not-inspired-by-*Alien* creature batted her sword away, but halted its attack, turning to focus on the swordswoman. Grognard hefted his glaive-guisarme and took a swing at the creature. The insect abomination ducked, and the three of them moved to encircle the creature.

Ree wished she had some thicker armor, especially when a claw swipe tore her apron in half, dropping the phaser to the floor. As soon as it hit the ground, the phaser started firing wildly. The three geeks scattered to the ground to avoid the blasts.

The bug-beast bounded over the table where Ree had taken cover, but it managed to jump right onto the blade of the lightsaber, which Ree'd held up over her head.

Ree's fortuitous duck-and-cover: 1
Bug Thing: 0.
Advantage: Reyes.

Ree, Grognard, Talon, and Chandra held off the randomly spawned creatures while ducking the erratic fire from assorted weaponry. Drake emerged from the back room with a device that looked like the unholy offspring of a Hookah and a vacuum tube television.

Drake set the machine down behind one of the tables and started unfolding a set of four chrome legs, each ending in a polished claw-foot. "Once I activate this, it may be best to keep your own magical tools out of the directional input valve."

"And that looks like what, exactly?" Ree asked, gesturing to the assortment of pipes, valves, and thingamabobs coming out of the machine.

He wiggled an opening that looked suspiciously like the store's vacuum cleaner's wide nozzle. "This one."

"Got it," Ree said, taking a step back.

Drake spooled up the device, which made a sucking sound that Ree didn't hear with her ears as much as with her . . . soul, maybe? Whatever it was, it felt woogy.

Whoa. Ree flashed back to the hoary days of smoking pot in college, though that might have been inspired by the Hookah shape as much as the existential tugging of the machine.

A *Space Samurai* freighter model came soaring over toward the bar, then dropped out of the air like an anvil when it crossed the plane of the machine's nozzle. Grognard dove forward, dropping the glaive to catch the model. He hit the ground with an "oof!" but kept the ship aloft.

He sidestepped back out of the beam's path and set the mini on the bar. "That thing costs $900."

Ree watched as more creatures, props, and game pieces wobbled under the power of Drake's machine. Plastic fighter squadrons clattered to the floor, war game figures holding skirmishes on Styrofoam terrain went still, and summoned creatures vanished back into the boxed sets, comics, and game books that were their origins.

For a moment, the room was still again.

"Thank fucking God," Ree said.

Grognard walked over to the store section, running his hand

over broken pieces, crumpled boxes, and mangled comics. Ree trotted over to join in as he surveyed the damage.

The devastation was near-total. Some of the weapons were still intact, but most had nicks, burns, or gouges taken out of the blades. The neat rows of comics had been mauled, trampled, burned, and scattered. Shelves and shelves of games had been wrecked, turned into a ruined mound of plastic sprues, torn cardboard tokens, and stained rulebooks.

Hundreds of games, figures, statuettes—each designed to bring joy, hone the mind, or celebrate passion for a story or a beloved character. All ruined. Ree felt sick to her stomach.

Grognard didn't talk, he just walked up and down the rows, taking it all in. Ree knew he did most of his inventory by memory, his mind an epic-level spreadsheet that rivaled the Overstreet Comics Price Guide.

The storeowner stopped at the end of a row, beside shattered glass cases with ruined busts and maquettes of superheroines, cyborgs, and starship captains. "I'm going to kill her," he said finally.

"Boss?" Ree asked.

His eyes were damp, shot through with red. "I'm going to find Lucretia, and I'm going to kill her myself. I can't recover from this," he said, opening his hands to the room. "At least two-thirds of the stock is completely ruined. And there's no way any insurance company is going to accept a vandalism claim when there's no evidence of forced entry, there are no suspects, and it took place while we were all here."

"When we find Lucretia, we can make her fix it," Ree said, even though she knew it was crap as she said it. "Or at least make her pay you back."

Eastwood joined them in the store. He looked at Grognard, the bags under his eyes even heavier when he was mostly back lit. "I'm . . . I'm sorry, Grognard. If I'd known . . ."

Grognard cut him off. "You didn't. It's her fault, no one else's. Help me get everyone out of this and find Lucretia.

That's all I need right now." The bearded geek nodded, and the two men shared the silent solidarity of the stoic male. Or something. Neither of them were the talk-about-our-feelings type.

Ree looked back to Drake's machine, which was vibrating and looked like it was being lit from within. "Do we need to worry about that thing exploding?" she asked.

"Of course not," Drake said. "Probably. Probably not. It might be best to find another use for this energy, just to be certain."

Grognard chuffed. "Just put it in the closet for now. We've got a bullfight to finish first. He picked through the piles of ruined merch and pulled out the Hulk hands he'd asked Ree to fetch before the store had gone gonzo. He picked them up, squeezed the foam a bit, and nodded. "Still good. You all can cover me, and I'll put this thing to bed. Then we can hunt down that haughty Nabokov fetishist and settle the books."

Grognard looked in turn to each of the geeks. "When I built this place, I knew that not everyone would like it, or me. That wasn't the point. The point was to make a place where we could be more than a bunch of bizarre obsessives in our little bolt-holes, where we could build a community, remember the things we share, and let off some steam. And no one is going to keep me from salvaging that dream, if there's anything left to it."

The rest of the group stood up, each with a bit more spring in their step. Except for Lieutenant Wickham, who had her back turned to Grognard and was intently staring at her iPad.

"Still can't beat that level on *Angry Birds*?" Ree asked.

Wickham didn't turn, just flipped Ree the bird.

Ree chuckled, then turned to Grognard. "Boss, you should let me use the Hulk hands," she said under her breath, trying not to draw attention to the request.

Grognard raised an eyebrow at her. "Why? The gloves are magic, but there's a baseline mass question, which means it should be me."

"Anyone can use the Adamantium Ale. And I can layer Buffy strength on with the Hulk hands," Ree said.

"This is my shop, Ree. And the woman who ruined it is on the other side of that Minotaur somewhere. It needs to be me."

Ree sighed. She could press the issue, maybe even win, but she could see the hurt in his eyes, something she'd never seen before in her sturdy boss. His world had been shaken to the core. He needed a win more, even if she might be able to pull off the deed more easily.

"In that case, you're going to need a clown to distract that thing and whatever else is out there."

That at least got a hint of a smile from the brewmaster. "I suppose I will."

Ree beamed, then pulled out her phone again, glad for the hundredth time that she'd shelled out for the Physical Resistance case.

She restarted the *Spider-Man* clip, and without the whirlwind of weird, she dropped into the fun of the film easily, filling her mind with the excitement of Spidey swinging his way around New York, strength, agility, and Spider-Sense all working in concert as Peter zoomed through the city.

When she looked up from the clip, she saw that Chandra, Drake, Eastwood, and Grognard had assembled by the door. Grognard was wearing the Hulk hands, and now that they were active, they'd changed from immobile foam fists into extensions of his hands, empowering his grip. He slammed one fist into an open hand, and each punch made its own mini thunderclap.

"Everyone ready?" Grognard asked. Ree picked up a Sting prop, spun it a few times in one hand to test the blade, and felt that it still had some power to it—some of the collective nostalgia for and love of the weapon in the Peter Jackson movie lingering in the prop.

She joined the ersatz adventuring party by the door, where Eastwood was pleading with Grognard to take the lead against the Minotaur.

"This is all because of me, Grognard," Eastwood said. "Let me take the gloves and set things right. It's the least I can do."

Grognard shook his head. "This discussion was over five minutes ago. Just keep everything else off of me while I put this animal down."

Ree saw that Wickham had moved over to give herself a better view of the coming chaos.

Standing just a few feet away, she felt the vibration of the door each time the Minotaur hit it, tirelessly hammering on the refreshed wards.

"Is that thing part Energizer bunny or what?" she said, trying to break the tension. Only Drake gave her a polite smile, the one he gave to be gracious, not because what she'd said was actually funny.

Not all of them can be gold, Ree admitted, and adjusted her grip on Sting, the *Spider-Man* energy still buzzing softly in her mind. She might get a good two minutes of fight out of the clip, depending on how much oh-shit last-second dodging she'd be doing.

Eastwood held the wrought-iron door ring in one hand, and counted down on fingers.

Three.

Two.

One.

CHAPTER SEVEN

The Bruce Banner Guide to Bull Fighting

"**G**o!" Grognard shouted as Eastwood threw open the door and they dove back into the tunnel.

Eastwood's glow sticks still lit the tunnel in water-tinted yellow light. Shadows played off the tunnel walls as dozens of shapes moved outside the door.

While Ree and company were busy with the storm, the Minotaur had brought some friends.

A dozen or so gnomes had returned, some clutching broken limbs or bloodied faces. Along with them were a handful of reptilian creatures that looked like crocodiles mixed with pit bulls—they had thicker bodies, stubby legs with knee joints that stuck straight out like a bulldog's, and forked tails.

Ree didn't even have time to gripe before Grognard leapt forward with a growl, leading with his Hulk hands. The Minotaur slashed with its axe, but Grognard swatted it aside with incredible strength and kept going for the creature's nose ring. The destruction of his store had lit jet fuel in his blood, and nothing was going to stop him.

Glad I didn't try to insist, Ree thought. She stepped into the tunnel and contorted her left hand to unload a burst of webbing at a cluster of gnomes and one of the bull-crocs. The netting hit and stuck the creatures together, collapsing into the murky water that sat in the base of the tunnel. Ree jumped up onto the opposite side of the tunnel, then dove blade-first at another bull-croc, burying the blade to the hilt in between the creature's shoulders before it could turn to face her.

The Minotaur was flailing around, stomping back and forth and slamming into the wall. The rumbles of vibration filled the tunnel, and yellow-gray snow fell around her as dust shook free from the old construction.

Go down already! she wanted to shout at the creature. But if she drew its attention back this way, Grognard would have to crawl over the creature's back to get to the nose ring.

Ree shot a burst of webbing at the Minotaur's feet, hoping to pin it down long enough for Grognard to rip the ring free and remove the creature's protections so she could backstab the thing for x4 damage and end this nightmare of a shift. The first web wrapped around the creature's fire-hydrant-size hoof and stuck it to the concrete walkway.

She saw Grognard laid out with a huge swing of the Minotaur's axe, folding the chain mail into his Lacuna Coil tour shirt. Her magical charge was nearly spent, but she shot another burst of webbing to pin the creature's other leg, keeping it from following up.

"Get him away from that thing!" Ree shouted.

All of a sudden, she fell into shadow as the Minotaur turned and loomed over her, showing a bloodied nose and a face that made hamburger look good. The creature tore through the webbing before it could settle, leaving it free to pivot like a homicidal Bulls mascot.

Eeep. Well, nothing left but bad ideas. Ree rammed Sting into the Minotaur's right arm, then used the sword as a handhold and did her best howler monkey impression, climbing up the side of the creature until she was perched on the creature's shoulder.

And because she had learned to take precautions, she pulled out the Ring of Giant Strength she'd pocketed from Grognard's case, slipped it onto her finger, then dove over the Minotaur's shoulder, catching herself on the nose ring. All of her body weight plus her enhanced strength hauled on the ring, and she felt something tear in the creature's nose. But it didn't come loose.

"Dogpile, now!" Ree said as the Minotaur started to flail, whipping her around like a dog with a toy. Her stomach simultaneously tried to escape out her toes while threatening to defy centrifugal force and come back up her throat. *Eeuuuccch.*

Remembering long nights at the county fair riding the Whirl & Hurl, she tucked her legs up and then did an inverted sit-up, crouching against the creature's face while the rest of the crew bound the axe down so it couldn't take her head off. Springing off the creature's chest, Ree wrenched with her ring-enhanced strength and ripped the nose ring off.

Consequently, this sent her flying straight into the wall.

Ree did her best to go limp, but she hit the concrete with the force of a thirty-foot fall. Pain cascaded across her body, rippling back and forth from a half-dozen spots.

For some long black moment, all she felt was pain. She heard shuffling, screaming, yelling, and the clash of blades, but mostly, she sputtered in bone-cracking agony.

A shadow fell over her, but this one came without the imminent sense of doom. Or maybe that was the shock settling in.

"Ree?" asked a voice. Ree focused on breathing, but her ribs felt like they'd collapsed into a jagged pile of lung-shredding shrapnel.

She opened her eyes, and saw a brownish blur, but not a fuzzy one. She felt a gloved hand touch her face softly, and then she blacked out.

Ree woke up feeling three-quarters dead. She tried to move, and her whole body was numb and cold.

She blinked her eyes open and saw the flat gray ceiling of Grognard's, only identifiable because of that odd red-brown stain the shape of a classic Base Star.

"Did anyone get the name of that wall?" Ree asked, the world wobbling as she tried to sit up.

"It would be best to keep resting, Ree," Drake said from her left.

Ree settled back against the floor? Table? And talked with her eyes closed.

"Is Grognard all right?"

"The drink kept the blow from being fatal. But we had to use extensive magical healing on both of you. Eastwood gave a detailed explication on metaphysical endurance limits and physio-spiritual strain. It was quite fascinating."

"What's that mean when it's in English?" Ree asked.

"Your body has been greatly taxed by the repeated magical healing. He said you should expect substantial fatigue, low core temperatures, and disorientation."

"Three for three," Ree said, bringing her hands up to massage her temple. Where she expected to find her glasses, she felt something else, larger, that covered her eyes. *Goggles, maybe?*

"Where are my glasses?" Ree asked.

"We think they're still in the tunnel. When we pulled you back inside, they were gone. I adjusted these goggles to your prescription," Drake offered.

"Should I ask how you did that?"

"If you like. The goggles were designed with medical as well as tactical applications. It was a simple modification."

"Did we get the Minotaur at least?" she asked, hoping the run had been worth it.

"The beast has been dispatched. But from the sounds, there are more creatures remaining." Drake sighed. "I would be impressed by Lady Lucretia's resourcefulness were it not currently leveled at us as artillery."

Ree tried to roll over onto her side. Her whole body was on pins, like a limb that fell asleep and then stung when you started it going again. "She's a regular bad luck ninja. Did Eastwood say when I'd be back on my feet?"

"You should be able to move shortly. Fighting may be another matter."

"Unless our visitors decide to bugger off, we don't have much of a choice."

"There's always a choice, Ree," Drake said, his voice kind. "It just so happens that we appear to be bereft of favorable options at this juncture."

Again, Ree wished that Drake and Priya had not met at that Steampunk salon, that they had not hit it off, and that somehow Priya was not one of her best friends. Then she could get with the smooching already. Honest, smart men with strong jaws and genuine smiles weren't in great supply anywhere, especially ones who could shoot, fight, and cobble together devices that thumbed their nose at the laws of physics.

Stow the pining, Reyes, she told herself. She gritted her teeth and sat up to take a look around the room.

Grognard was laid out on the floor ten feet away, his chain-mail coat rent open across the chest, dried blood crusted onto his shirt.

Chandra and Talon sat at a nearby table. Chandra held a bundle wrapped in a bar towel to her side, and Talon's shoulder was wrapped in bandages. Three empty bottles sat on the table, as well as two half-drunk pints.

Uncle Joe sat at another table, fiddling with several stacks of cards. His hair was matted with blood, and the left leg of his jeans ended below the knee, revealing bandages wrapped from his calf down to his ankle.

Eastwood paced the store. His coat was off, and she saw cuts up and down his arms, sealed over (probably with magic), but not bandaged. She stopped to pick up a prop wand, tested it for a second, then walked it back to the bar area and set the wand on a table that stood beside the steps between the bar and the store. It joined a small stack of other props—a dagger, the Sting replica, an *Aliens*-style pulse rifle, and several others that Ree couldn't pin down unless she got closer. The goggles worked just fine, but they felt weird, even through her dulled sense of touch.

Ree looked back to the bar, expecting a sloppily drunk Wickham, but she was gone. Ree scanned the rest of the room, but didn't see her anywhere.

"Where's Wickham?" Ree asked.

Drake shook his head. "She's gone. It appears that she took the confusion as her opportunity to slip away and take her chance in the sewers. Perhaps if we're all fortunate, the gnomes have taken her to be their plaything."

"At least she's finally gone."

There was a groaning sound, and Ree turned to see Grognard fumbling into consciousness. She walked, gingerly, over to her boss and knelt down to help him as Drake had helped her.

"You're safe, boss. We're inside," Ree said, a soft hand on the brewmaster's shoulder.

"How many bottles did you use?" Grognard asked, rubbing at his head, likely as fuzzy as Ree was.

Ree looked up to the others, who consulted between themselves for a few moments.

"Nine. Three for you, three for Ree, one each for the rest of us," Chandra said.

Grognard nodded slowly. "Someone please tell me we got that bastard."

"Done and done. But there's plenty of company left outside," Ree said.

Grognard sat up, and blinked several times. He started to pick himself up, and Ree offered her hand, leaning back as the big man rose to his feet.

"Then we've got to put this to bed." The shopkeep looked

around, to the pile of props on the table, and then over to Drake's contraption.

"That thing is still charged, right?" he asked.

Drake nodded. "Indeed. It will need a siphon to shunt off the charge soon."

Grognard smiled, as if Drake had said exactly what the big man wanted to hear. "I've got an idea. Bet it'll take some tinkering, though. Think you could hook that thing up to one of my brewing vats?"

Drake quirked an eyebrow. "For what purpose?"

"When you and Ree lost the cart, I decided to try out a new recipe. It needs to age a bit more, but if we rig that thing up right, we might be able to speed up the brewing and get ourselves a game-winner without having to wade out into that bullshit again." Grognard waved dismissively at the door and the infrequent thumps, *thud*s, and weakening *zot*s of magical backlash.

"How exactly will that work?" Ree asked. She noticed that Eastwood had fallen in beside her, several feet off to her right. Close enough to be in the conversation but not so close that he got into anyone's bubble.

"Inspector Gadget and I can take care of that. Everyone else needs to keep those things outside long enough for us to make it work."

Ree looked to Talon, Chandra, and Uncle Joe, who tensed up. None of them were fresh, and their arsenals were getting thin.

"We can do this, Ree," Eastwood said from beside her. She looked to the bearded geek and saw determination on his face. Not the self-destructive bravery that had been his default for most of the past year, just a tired certainty. As he slipped his trench coat back on, she couldn't help but think of it as Grit.

Ree pointed at the door. "This, yes. But that doesn't mean I'm in on your plan," she said, rehashing the argument that had started their evening.

Eastwood nodded in a conceding-the-point kind of way. "Never thought it did. Lucretia first, then we can figure out how to get Branwen. We're on the same side. Always have been." Eastwood paused as Ree started to roll her eyes. He raised a hand to hold off her doubt. "Except when I went off the rails. You can trust me."

Conflicting impulses threw a mosh pit in Ree's gut, turning into a cartoon dust cloud with arms and legs sticking out as it rampaged across her emotional landscape. She wanted to deck Eastwood, hug him, and get drunk all at once.

And the whole time, the long-suffering door shuddered under the constant assault from outside.

Chandra, Talon, and Uncle Joe fell in, completing a circle with Ree and Eastwood by the door.

"Are we going back out there?" Uncle Joe asked, looking at his feet. Something in the end of the last melee had shattered his hard-won confidence, and he was back to the nervous collector she'd always known.

Talon was loaded for bear, longsword at her hip, a smaller blade over her shoulder, and throwing knives strapped to her hip opposite the scabbarded sword. In her hands, she held the naginata. She looked like an advertisement for *Diablo III*. Ree wanted to take a picture and post it on Tumblr. Unlike Joe, Talon—battered but unbroken—still had the fire in her eyes.

Chandra was somewhere in the middle—she looked hurt, and she was clearly running on empty, living in that place where you keep going on willpower until you've got nothing left to give. The punk Geekomancer held a kukri strapped to her hip and clutched the *Aliens* pulse rifle like it was a shiny, ass-kicking baby.

"If we go out, we need to plan for as many eventualities as we can," Ree said. "We can assume there will be more gnomes, and maybe some of those bulldog crocodile things. But there could be more bruisers, and Lucretia herself."

Nods all around.

Chandra spoke up. "We'd cleared out about half of what was outside when we dragged you two inside, but there was still one of the croc things, and about a dozen gnomes. It sounds like there are more now."

"So we start with AoE from the door. Joe, that's all you."

The older man didn't so much nod as bob up and down, rocking back and forth slightly.

He won't last another fight, Ree thought. But she'd thought that last time, too.

"Joe, you stay inside. We can toss out some pain from the door, but there's no need for everyone to dive out there if we don't need to. Plus, someone has to be able to signal Drake and Grognard if things break bad. Sound good?"

Uncle Joe's relief was palatable. He shrugged off twenty pounds of worry, his face brightening. "I can do that."

"Talon, you'll need to be anchor, keep them out of the door and at arm's length whenever possible. They can't be allowed to swarm us when we're trying to fight ranged."

Talon spun the haft of her naginata. "Got it. Just like the Bridge Battle at Pennsic."

"I'll take your word on that," Ree said with a smile. She'd never been, herself, but hoped that Talon would keep delivering.

"Chandra, I say you use that rifle until it gives up the ghost. Follow up Joe's AoE with some suppressive fire as we get out into the tunnel, then mow them down. Let us know when the gun's dry."

Ree turned to Eastwood. "Eastwood, Smash." That got chuckles all around. She didn't need to tell him what to do. To hear him tell the tales, he'd been living the life since Ree was in grade school. He fought like a man possessed. Dude would be fine.

"Everybody good?" Ree asked. She scanned the group, looking for questions, but mostly, for doubt. Doubt in her, the plan, or whatever.

Somewhere along the way, I became the leader, Ree realized.

That's what she got for being Grognard's right hand, the Ivanova to his Sinclair (he was too stoic to be Captain Chuckles).

"Let's go," Ree said, and turned to the door, doing her best to tap into Ivanova's confidence and epic badassery, even if she didn't have the time to do it for real. But magic or no, Ivanova was a role model, and today, Ree would try to do both her and Grognard proud.

Ree hauled the door open about a foot, and then braced her shoulder to keep it from busting open.

She saw Uncle Joe tossing cards, and for another moment, he was a hero, a latter-day Gambit raining playing-card hell on his enemies. She heard a firecracker rumble of several explosions, tortured screams from gnomes and other less-human voices.

After ten seconds of furious card-flopping, Uncle Joe stepped back and Chandra took his place, unloading with the pulse rifle.

"You like that, you sons of bastards! Woooh!" Chandra's eyes grew wide with fury as she unloaded into the crowd.

That should be all the opening we need. Ree pulled open the door and let it swing past her.

"Close this behind us, and listen!" she told Joe in a stage bellow, taking up her lightsaber and pushing forward with Eastwood and Talon.

Several mounds of dead gnomes and other creatures were smoldering in the sewer, not yet popped to ichor. But there were plenty of bogies left in the neighborhood. More gnomes rushed forward, and Ree flipped her lightsaber on to spear through two of them mid-jump. Ree stepped to the side and the creatures fell in two pieces behind her. She kicked another gnome, then brought the lightsaber back through two more as they rushed in to overwhelm her.

The weapon wouldn't last long, since it'd been used heavily and there hadn't been much time for it to recharge, maybe an hour in total. So she had to cause maximum damage in minimum time. She spun through the creatures, blade always moving, a flowing techno-trance dance of death and dismemberment.

It was awesome. She'd reached that place beyond exhaustion, that place she found sometimes at work, sometimes out dancing, and all too often in her wacky adventures. That place where the conscious mind had buggered off to sleep and all that was left was pure instinct and muscle memory, action driven by necessity. She'd fight and win, or she'd die.

So she fought.

Keeping her dance flurry going, she turned and Greater Cleave-d her way back to the others, where Eastwood was dancing his own Pwntentantz. Where Ree was fighting with her best Ataru-esque form, melding her Taekwondo and other martial arts experience into an all-speed-all-the-time fight, Eastwood was kicking it old-school, reminiscent of Obi-Wan Kenobi. He stood his ground, the enemy moved around him, and then fell still. When he did move, it was in fits and bursts, deceptively fast.

In the middle, Talon swung the naginata around like it weighed nothing. She speared one of the bull-crocs through the jaw, then raised the haft of the naginata to block the swings of several skeletal creatures who fought with rusty machetes. She pulled out a hammer that Ree hadn't even seen and smashed in one skeleton's skull. Then kicked the other one right into the swing of Ree's lightsaber.

If we keep this up, we might just get out of here. The enemy's ranks were thinning. She could pick a way through the gnomes on both sides of the tunnel.

Famous last words.

Just as she started to wonder which way they'd need to go to track down Lucretia, she heard the sound of a steam engine.

"What's that?" Talon asked.

"Good question." Ree cut through several more gnomes, then dodged to the side as another skeleton hacked down with a rusty blade. She slid her leg between the construct's, then leaned in, knocking the creature off its balance and sending it toppling into the sewage. That bought her the time to jump off the ledge, stomp the skeleton's skull in, then take another gnome out at the waist.

And then, as a whistle echoed down the hall, her lightsaber gave up the Force ghost, the weapon growing light and still, back to being just a high-end prop.

The gnomes wasted no time. Two jumped at her in concert, using their temporary height advantage to make for her face. She ducked and dodged left, reaching out with a jabbing punch to hit one in the gut. The other landed on her side, digging in as it climbed on her with all four limbs like a homicidal beast.

Ree spun with the extra weight, and reached over to pull the creature off her shoulder. Its claws bit in again as she pulled it off and slammed it into the concrete ledge. The gnome she'd punched came again. Facing only one this time, she reached around its spindly arm and yanked, sending the creature off course and tumbling to the ground at her side.

That move she'd picked up from an aikido instructor. It was also a babysitting hack, a way for dealing with aggressive kids without hurting them. The gnomes made those kids look like little cherubs.

There was another whistle, and Ree turned to see a ramshackle cart rolling its way toward them, one wheel each on the ledges that lined the tunnels. It had a mini-ballista of a crossbow mounted to the front, and held a trio of green-brown-skinned goblins. The goblins had wide, pointed ears and the large eyes of the Pathfinder RPG versions, which meant that they were just smart enough to be dangerous. Though that didn't explain where they'd picked up the *Chitty Chitty Bang Bang* war machine.

"Incoming!" Ree shouted. She pulled out her phaser, which was probably also running close to empty. She fired on the contraption, clipping one of the goblins. The creature dropped out of view, but not before a goblin with aviator-style goggles fired the mini-ballista. A baseball-bat-size bolt shot at her, and the only way for Ree to dodge was down.

She took a deep gulp and dropped prone, into the still muck and ichor of the fallen monsters.

Ewewewewewewewew, Ree thought, then pulled herself out of the muck, fighting the sticky suction. *Well, at least I was wearing goggles,* she admitted, wiping the sewage off the lenses as she rushed forward to get onto or under the contraption before it could fire again. If she'd gotten some of that in her eye, it'd take an hour in a medical shower and a fifth of tequila to wash it off.

She fired the phaser at the ballista, but the movement threw off her aim, and she just caught a wooden box to the side, which was either some kind of support or a step for the diminutive drivers.

The two remaining goblins were cranking the ballista back into a ready position, but they were only ten paces out. Ree fired again with the phaser and hit a goblin square in the chest, but the beam cut off as soon as it hit, the weapon going dead. Five paces out, she drew the switchblade from her soaked apron and flipped it open as she jumped up to the ledge on her left, then jumped for the goggled goblin, leading with her knife. The creature ducked, cursing in a language that sounded like a mix of *Mars Attacks!* Martian and Gaelic.

Ree overshot the goblin, but landed on the rickety cart. She grabbed onto the cart with her free hand and tried to flip back around to face the goblin. The creature was on her as she turned, and she found herself grappling with a bitey-scratchy-dirty thing for at least the tenth time that night. But even her average strength let her overpower the goblin, and her knife struck home.

The goblin stopped struggling, and she dropped it from her blade and then tried to figure out how to stop the cart.

There were levers, switches, and gauges all over, none of them labeled. And the only lighting was from the dim lights in the roof of the tunnel.

For lack of a better option, she tried to repeat what had happened to Grognard's cart just a month earlier. She rocked back and forth, moving the cart with her. Then she jumped straight up, grabbed the cart as it rocked to the right, and pulled that direction with all her weight. The cart lurched, then pitched and rolled down into the central muck. The wooden cart cracked, and spindled itself into a wreck as the engine of the cart tried to keep moving.

Well, that's done, Ree thought, sighing from the muck. A wall of fatigue hit her with the sigh, and she had to force herself forward, sloshing back toward the door and her compatriots . . . whom she had left on their own when she'd spotted the cart.

Eastwood's glow sticks still shone yellow, refracting through the mulch to illuminate the twenty feet of tunnel around the door to Grognard's shop.

Eastwood, Talon, and Chandra were backed against the door by a cloud of animated weapons. Axes, swords, knives, maces, and more flew around one another, slashing and hacking at the group, moving on their own.

Huh. Don't see that every day, Ree thought, flashing back to magic swords that flew around and fought on their own in *D&D.* But she'd never seen that many all at once, a golem of animated blades.

And all she had was a knife. Talon was parrying with unreal skill, warding off three of the weapons at any given time. Eastwood's lightsaber was out of sight, and he fought with a long German dagger. Chandra shuffled to the side, but a longsword arced out from the center of the cloud, cutting into her path and forcing her back.

But why hasn't it gone in for the kill? Ree asked herself.

Using her meager momentum, Ree jumped over to the opposite side of the tunnel, and came in to flank the weapon cloud, for all the good that would do. When she got close enough, the longsword spun around and sliced out at her, the rest of the cloud following.

"Get back inside!" Ree said, backpedaling to try and outrun the flying tsunami of weaponry.

"What about you?" Talon asked.

Ree's knife more of a liability than a defense—parrying wasn't an option. It was all-dodge, all-the-time. And she was already tired. Every juke and duck required her to dig deeper, and she didn't know how much she had left before the shovel of her determination would hit the hard slate of burnout. "It'll be easier for you to sneak me inside once you're inside, right? Get a shield to ward this thing off."

Ree ducked, hopped, and jogged out of the way of the weapon cloud as Chandra and Talon made their way back inside. Eastwood tried to bait the cloud himself, hacking at blades and hafts with his long knife. But the cloud had apparently decided on going after the muck-soaked skinny chick instead of the merely ambiently stinky scruffy-looking guy.

"Hey! Oy! Come at me, gorramit!" Eastwood said, laying into the far side of the weapon cloud as Ree huffed, keeping a quarter step ahead of the whirling blades.

The blades turned, and pressed in at Eastwood, backing him against the wall by the door. Ree's lungs threatened to collapse in on themselves and lock the alveoli shut, so she stumbled as she moved forward to help Eastwood.

Through the cloud of weapons, she saw several plumes of blood and a tattooed arm. Then Eastwood disappeared.

Leaving her alone in the tunnel with the cloud of weapons, on the wrong side of the tunnel from any backup, and completely unable to breathe.

Fuck.

CHAPTER EIGHT

The Right Hand of Vengeance

As her mind raced to figure out a way to get past the cloud of whirling weapons, Ree heard a voice from inside.

"Talon coming out!"

The door opened just enough for the warrior woman to slide out, leading with the huge scutum. The shield was big enough to cover both women . . . assuming Ree could get to her without becoming a pincushion.

"I'm running on fumes here," Ree said, hyperventilating just to try to get her lungs to bellow. She knew it was the exact opposite of the best thing to do, but desperation and exhaustion had teamed up on discipline and were winning handily.

Talon shield-bashed the cloud of weapons, then shuffled to the side and hustled over to Ree. The big woman hauled Ree's arm over her shoulder, then pulled her along as the cloud of weapons hacked, stabbed, and hammered away at the scutum.

Ree focused on putting one foot in front of the other, with a side of trying to keep her lungs from jumping out her throat and ballooning their way to Paradise Falls.

One of the blows knocked the both of them against the wall, and several overhand cuts glanced off of Ree's skull.

When did I go to the salon? Ree asked herself, the world getting very far away.

She felt a hailstorm of blows against the shield, then heard a mess of voices and smelled a gust of fresher air. Finally, she heard the slamming of a door and the clattering of something large hit the ground. Then she joined it.

⋅✕⋅⬡⋅✕⋅

The original series Base Star welcomed her back to consciousness. Someone pressed a hot mug into her hands.

"Drink this."

Warm hands raised the mug to her mouth, and she drank. The whatever-it-was tasted awful. A familiar awful, though. She opened her eyes and saw Drake holding her hands and the mug, grease smeared on his face and in his hair.

"Is this that make-your-soul-better goop?" Ree asked, her voice coming out froggy. He'd made a gallon of it for her the first time they'd gone into the Spirit realm. It tasted like ass juice but worked wonders.

"That it is. It should ameliorate some of the fatigue."

Ree held her nose closed and took another long drink from the mug. The wretched taste fell back a bit with longer gulps, though only from a rating of "puke my guts out" to "this may no longer be food."

She released her nose and took a few halting breaths before downing the rest of the disgusting tea. She'd once asked Drake what was in it, and he'd promptly changed the subject. It was probably for the best.

The tea kicked in fast, the rest of her body waking up, warmed like she'd just had a hot bath. Ree looked around, and saw Talon and Eastwood bracing against the door, Chandra standing a pace behind them with a crossbow at the ready.

The door shook under regular blows, and once again, the *zot* of Grognard's wards was gone. There were several gouges in the door, and Ree saw several dozen shredded cards on the floor by the entranceway.

"How long until the brew is ready?" Ree asked.

"Still another half-hour. The intermediary step of channeling the energy into a device to speed the fermentation process has only a thirty-seven percent efficiency rate, and that was after making several aggressive modifications, and several trial-and-error cycles." Drake gestured to his grease-stained and singed clothes. His left sleeve ended just below the left shoulder, and his pants looked . . . crispy.

"But it'll work?" she asked.

Drake pursed his lips. "I doubt that we will have sufficient time for a field test. Eastwood informs me that the door may not last until the brew is ready."

Ree sat up, wobbled, then found her feet. "Then we have to get back out there and thin the herd again." It's not like there were many other options.

When forced to choose between "fight and maybe live," and "wait and probably die," Ree was finding that the former was always better. At least then she was doing something instead of sitting on her hands and praying for the cavalry to arrive. Especially since her normal cavalry was all already there.

The tea had helped, but she still felt like death warmed over.

"Where's my phone?" she asked. She left it inside before each sortie, since even with a mondo-tough case, it wasn't going to stand up to the beatings she went through.

But since Eastwood, Talon, and Chandra were a little busy, only Drake was really present to answer, and he didn't seem to know. She searched through the St. Patty's Day–level mess in the bar and found the phone underneath a torn half of a *Fantastic Four* comic.

Clicking the phone on, Ree saw that she had 23% left on the battery. It'd be enough for two more doses of power, maybe three. But going the *Spider-Man* or *Buffy* route again wasn't going to cut it. She needed to think non-Euclidean, get sneaky on the situation. Every single time they'd gone out to clean house, Lucretia had answered with another wave of nasty, and it didn't seem like she was running low on cannon fodder.

So what, then? Ree thought, browsing her media list.

It didn't seem to matter what power she had, they would just keep coming. So either she needed to get past them and find Lucretia, which would mean leaving the rest of the group another person down, or she had to change the way that she fought.

She scrolled past clips of superheroes, detectives, psychics, and chosen ones.

And found herself a winner.

The last fights had all been about endurance, about pressing on no matter what happened.

She didn't need super-power; she needed staying power.

Ree plopped onto a chair by the nearly bare weapons table and fired up a clip from *Die Hard*. John McClane, the patron saint of action heroes, the man whose ingenuity, inexorable will, and smart-assery had carried him through endless trials and launched Bruce Willis's seemingly unkillable career as an action hero.

She'd picked out two clips from *Die Hard* for her power playlist. One for his MacGyver-ness (taping the gun to his back), and one for his indomitable will (walking across broken glass). She played the latter, and did her best to feel McClane's pain, use it to fuel her own determination, make the hero's will her own. Internal powers seemed to last longer than the external, flashy stuff. If she could dig into *Die Hard* well enough, she should be able to fight on even through the exhaustion of a dozen skirmishes on top of working on her feet for six hours.

Die Hard had, for Ree, opened the doors for action movies where it actually seemed like the hero was in pain, that he'd really struggled through, and that struggling made him all the more heroic. It was that grit she needed. The kind of grit that Eastwood had earned over years fighting in the astral plane of the World Wide Web, that Talon had earned on the battle-fields of Pennsic and Pearson both. Ree was still in her rookie year as an urban fantasy heroine. It seemed like she'd seen more than most in that time, but she needed to dig deeper than her reserves would allow, the way that McClane had.

The sound of cracking wood pulled Ree from her me-dia communion, and she accepted the jian straight-sword pressed into her hand by Drake.

"Good luck," he said, then dashed back into the office to join Grognard.

Ree stood, set her phone back on the table, then hustled over to the crew by the door, which now had a splintered head-size hole around shoulder level. A broad blade hacked into the wood again, widening the gap.

"Go time?" Ree asked as she stepped up.

"Go!" Eastwood said, undoing the locks as Talon stabbed back through the hole in the door with the naginata.

The door swung open, revealing another adventure mod-ule's worth of nastiness.

That would have normally been the time when her stom-ach sank at the vastness of the creatures' numbers, the skel-etons, gnomes, eagle-size winged lizards, and especially at the purple hippo (*WTF?*).

But not this time. This time, she had the determination of John McClane. The power of *Die Hard* was different from most of the others she'd taken on using Geekomancy. When she channeled Buffy, Trinity, or Spider-Man, she felt the power buzzing in her mind and in her body, always just right there waiting for her to tap into it. This was more like a solid sense of certainty, a cool well of confidence buoying her up.

I could get used to this, she thought.

Eastwood dove forward, lashing out with sword and long dagger. Ree pegged his style as the Niten-do of Musashi's

The Book of Five Rings, though he was using western weapons instead of the samurai's daisho.

Chandra followed, moving more cautiously than Eastwood, her kukri spinning in tight patterns.

Ree went third, letting Talon and her polearm take the anchor role behind them. Uncle Joe was on door duty, his well of courage properly spent.

Leading with the sword, Ree stabbed at one of the winged lizards, which pumped its wings and dodged up and away from her blow.

She followed the thrust with a cross-body cut, which caught a leaping gnome's arm and carried through to cut it across the collarbone. The diminutive devil went down, and Ree continued her swing, spinning her weapon back around to her right to ward off another gnome before it could jump.

If she let the blade stop moving, she'd get overrun. Already feeling her barely mustered energy flag, Ree dipped into that cool well of magical energy, thinking of how John McClane hadn't stopped, hadn't given up, had always pressed on.

For understandable reasons, "Ode to Joy" started playing in her head, making the fairly workmanlike task of cutting down scads of monsters seem instantly more epic.

But even with her epic soundtrack, they were outnumbered and out-gunned. (Out-sworded, really. All of the prop guns were spent, and Lucretia didn't seem to be a gun bunny.)

Just a few minutes. Just need to keep them from knocking down the door for a few minutes. Except that twenty minutes in fighting time was approximately forever. She'd competed in Taekwondo tournaments for years, and even those ninety-second matches dragged on like they were the battle of Helm's Deep.

"How are we going to keep this up?" Ree shouted to Eastwood. If the monsters understood her, then so be it. She knew she was screwed, and the monsters might well know it, too. There were just too many.

"Don't know!" Eastwood said, fighting on. "Just do it!"

Determined he was, but Eastwood was no speech giver. But he was holding his own, even though he'd lost the long knife somewhere along the way and was fighting with just the one sword and judiciously applied dirty tricks.

Pressed up against the wall, Chandra was favoring one leg. Beside her, Talon fought with her personal sword, a hand-and-a-half blade that she wielded like she'd had it since she was in diapers and baby tunics. And as a second-gen Scadian, that might even be the case.

Ree was drinking deeply of the *Die Hard* determination, but the creatures kept coming. The sewer channel was running with ichor, a stream of fallen monstrosities flowing away from the store, but not fast enough.

A boxy robot that looked like a teakettle on steroids launched forward, spout-butting her knee. She hopped back, lashing out with the sword, which sparked and clattered off the machine's domed top.

In the next minute, she heard several more cries of pain. Chandra went down, and Talon dropped to one knee, warding everything off of the fallen punk.

Which left Ree and Eastwood nearly alone against the pressing horde. If there had been more space, they'd have been overrun long ago. As it was, the four of them half stumbled over one another as they tried to keep the store side of the tunnel at their flanks so the creatures couldn't cut them off from the door. Ree took wounds along her arms, back, and legs. The *Die Hard* magic started to go faster and faster as she fought on with injuries that even adrenaline couldn't push through.

Talon screamed as an arrow embedded itself in her shoulder, then dropped out from Ree's peripheral vision.

This isn't going to work.

Ree adopted her best get-the-whole-damn-bar's-attention voice and shouted "Joe! Evac!" while pounding on the door with the pommel of her blade. Then she twisted the blade to spear another gnome as it leapt for her throat.

The door opened, and Ree held her ground, taking scratches and bruises under the ever-more-crowded press of monsters.

She heard wincing and pained moans behind her, which she hoped were Talon and Chandra getting their ass out of Dodge.

"You next!" Grognard said, the end of his word devolving into a growl as she heard steel tear leather and flesh.

She felt a blood-slicked hand reach out and push her backward. Eastwood filled the doorway, pressed on all sides. His coat turned aside some of the blows, but not nearly enough. Ree grabbed the geek by the collar as she felt something pulling her back, and the three of them toppled onto the cold concrete floor of Grognard's. She saw another spectral hand slam the door closed, breaking bones and severing limbs in a very un-cartoon-y fashion.

"Holy shit!" Ree said, the lack of immediate mortal danger reminding her just how many times she'd been stabbed, cut, and bludgeoned.

And they said I hit the healing limit last time. That's just fucking great.

Grognard was there, with glasses of water and his medical kit. She assumed Drake was still with the brew, working on their Hail Mary.

Eastwood did his best to brace the door while Grognard bandaged wounds with the rapidity of an EMT on speed.

"Were you a medic or something?" Ree asked as her boss tore off part of her pants to get at the wound along her shin. He washed the muck and blood out, then glopped so much antiseptic on it that Ree nearly shot straight up in the air.

"Something. You can wrap the arm yourself. And keep your head elevated."

"How's the beer bomb?" Ree asked, but Grognard had already moved on. Chandra and Talon were unresponsive, but looked like they were still breathing.

"Not ready," Eastwood said.

Ree looked at the door, where Eastwood was as much leaning on the door for support as bracing it against the hordes.

"Where did she get all of these things?" Ree asked.

"Lucretia has been at this for quite a while. Anyone who's been in the game keeps some resources back. But I didn't expect that she'd go this far, not for something that she frakking stole from me in the first place!"

Once More, with Feeling

A hundred fists hammered at the sturdy wood of the thick front door at Grognard's Grog and Games. Ree pressed her back against the door, her boots sliding on the smooth floor of the concrete, failing to find a good grip. The shop was a total wreck—games, cards, figures, and props scattered everywhere, drinks spilled across the bar, tables upended and shattered. Ree wanted to think that the gnomes couldn't make it much worse, but the "getting eaten alive" part banished that thought pretty fast.

"What the fuck has gotten into those little guys?" Ree asked. Pearson's sewer gnomes were already more like ghouls than the helpful creatures in *David the Gnome* or the curious tinkerers from *D&D*, but this was a whole new level of aggro.

Eastwood stood beside her, leaning into the door with one shoulder, cuts and bruises scored across his face and hands.

"Don't know, but we can't hold out long like this. And if they get in, we're *bantha pudu*."

Ree could feel the scraping and scratching at the door, then a louder *thud*.

That was no gnome. Ree took a millisecond to consider

what else might be out there, but it didn't really matter, since it probably wanted them dead just as much as the tiny creatures.

"How we doing back there?" Ree shouted to the back room.

"A short while longer, sad to say!" Drake answered, his voice hoarse.

Ree cursed under her breath. "We're not made of time out here. Either the gnomes have made themselves a battering ram, or there's a cave Troll out there!"

"It wouldn't be a cave Troll. They hate the smell down here. Sewer Troll, maybe," Eastwood said.

"Thanks, Mr. Monster Manual," Ree said, short temper unleashing the full power of her snark. "How does this help us not get dead?"

Beat.

"It doesn't," Eastwood admitted.

"Then I don't need to know. Hurry up, guys!" Ree shouted again.

Eastwood nudged her. "Get to a weapon. I've got this."

"That's preposterous. The door will cave in as soon as I move."

"Trust me. We need to be ready."

"I trust you, but I still think it's ridiculous."

"I'll take it," Eastwood said, pushing her away from the door.

What the fuck is it about Saturdays? Ree asked herself as she felt the door splintering behind her.

Ree looked to Uncle Joe. "Do you have anything left? For the door, for crowd control, anything?"

Joe flipped through his binders. Most of the pages were empty. "I lost most of the cards I had on consignment in the curse. This was just what I had on me."

"I don't need Serra Angels here. I'd take some Thallids, even."

Joe shook his head. "You don't want Thallids. The last time someone used Thallids, it ended up like VanderMeer's *Finch*."

"Didn't see that one. But we need something, Joe."

Joe pulled a card out of a sleeve, looking at it like it was his child. "If it's the only way."

"It's the only way!" Ree said as she felt splintering wood bite into her back. The *Die Hard* magic was almost gone, and she could feel world-annihilating fatigue at the edge of her mind.

"It's not the only way!" shouted Drake from the back. "The brew is ready!"

"Thank God," Uncle Joe said.

"Can you get it out here?" Ree shouted.

In response, Drake wheeled a cart with a glass jug filled with many gallons of a dark amber-brown liquid.

Grognard met Drake in the bar section and guided the jug over to the door.

"How exactly is this going to work?" Ree asked.

"The glass is warded against the effects of the beer," Grognard said, spinning the cart so that it would fit through the door. "But if we break it, it'll go off like an omnidirectional mine."

"Won't that take out the door, too?" Ree asked.

"That's why as soon as we shut the door, we run."

Ree's eyes went wide. "No one told me this plan involved running away from explosions and jumping at the last second to avoid getting killed."

"We're not rich with options here, kid," Grognard said.

He was right. The store was already ruined, and if they wanted to get out alive, it'd take something extreme.

She went over to help Drake drag Talon, Chandra, and Shade into the back room, where there'd be at least one more barrier between them and the explosion.

"So we're going to hide up in the wreckage there?" Ree asked, pointing at the game store section.

"Seems like," Grognard said.

They did their best to arrange the downed geeks as comfortably as possible in the back room, then jogged out toward the door.

The dramatic and fatalistic part of her mind wanted to do something cliché and grab Drake for one good smooch before they kicked the jug outside, but she was too tired for a grand gesture.

Down, girl. If getting one smooch is the only thing you can think to do before maybe dying, you're doing it wrong.

What she really wanted to do was write that letter to her dad. Or to the Rhyming Ladies, Bryan, and the Blins. Anyone, someone who would remember her as something other than the doomed barhand at Grognard's.

"Here goes nothing," Ree said, propping herself up on a table, the permanently borrowed jian by her side.

"No. You go that way," Eastwood said, gesturing to the store section. "This is a two-person job. You've done enough."

Ree's oppositional defiant impulses flared. She wanted to fight again. But he was right. There was no reason for them all to stand by waiting and then have to go running. This wasn't an action movie.

Eastwood held the door ready, and Grognard pushed the cart back and forth, building up momentum. Drake offered an arm to help Ree hobble over to the store section, where they took cover behind one of the overturned tables. Even after everything else, Drake still had his rifle at the ready, as if he'd actually be using it. Whatever version of Boy Scouts they had in Avalon were very impressive.

Grognard counted down, and after he called one, Eastwood pulled open the door. As he did, Grognard shoved the jug forward, his timing perfect. The cart picked up several creatures in its path, and Ree saw the whole thing go off the side of the walkway as the door slammed closed. Eastwood and Grognard dove one each to a side.

The subsequent *BOOM!* sounded strangely like the kind of burp you made after shotgunning a half-yard of beer. Not that Ree had any idea what that sounded like. Nope, she definitely hadn't made it herself back in college, followed by her being sick for a day and a half.

She was a writer, after all. Creative license. Definitely

not the other thing.

The explosion tore the door off its hinges, a plume of amber-brown flame gushing through the doorway and filling her vision of the bar section.

The wave of heat rolled over the table and dropped onto Ree like a five-ton cartoon weight. She dropped to the floor, huddling behind the table with Drake beside her.

But a moment later, the heat faded. She looked up over the table and saw the roof and floor of the bar scorched black.

But on either side were Eastwood and Grognard, shaking themselves out and wobbling to their feet.

And out the door, Ree saw nothing.

Not a fucking thing. For the first time in what seemed like forever. It had been maybe two hours, but it felt like she'd been in and out of that now-absent door for a week.

"Are they gone?" Ree asked as she and Drake hobbled back toward the bar.

Grognard stepped into the doorway. He looked left, and he looked right. And most important, nothing tackled, stabbed, or jumped him.

He put his hands on his hips. "Good riddance."

Ree fist-pumped, then regretted the action as it tore open one of her cuts. She strung together some dockhand-worthy obscenities but kept walking with Drake to the door.

"Next up, Lucretia," Eastwood said. His voice was determined, but he was a dead man walking. Each step looked like it cost him minutes off his life.

Grognard looked a bit better, but not much. Drake was in the best shape of any of them, only fairly bedraggled. She blamed it on his unflappable pseudo-Britishness.

"Are we quite certain that it is necessary to seek justice right now? We're hardly in any shape for another melee."

"After a stunt like this, she's not going to waltz into market and make herself an easy target," Grognard said. "We finish this . . . now."

"She can't have much left in her," Eastwood said, clearly trying to psych himself up. "Not after all that."

Ree mustered as much askance-itude as possible. "So we're just going to go stomping through the sewer, most of us dead on our feet, in the hopes that the person we're after doesn't have a contingency plan? It may be the concussions talking, but that sounds ludicrous."

Grognard growled. "She can't get away with this crap. Even half-dead, there're four of us." He looked at Uncle Joe. "Five if you want in. How much has she cost you tonight?"

A wave of pain passed over Joe's face. "I lost count at sixty-five hundred dollars."

"And?" Grognard asked, a question so leading it was close to stealing the next base.

Joe threw up his hands in frustration. "I'm down to crap commons and resource cards, man. I'm tapped out."

"If you won't go, I'll do this myself," Eastwood said, taking up the simple one-handed sword he'd been using since his lightsaber went out. He crossed to a mound of broken, bent, and mangled weapons, rummaging through the detritus to pull out a hand-size buckler.

What? It's not like you haven't done things just as inadvisable before, Ree told herself. But this felt different. It felt more like the Alamo or Marathon, despite the fact that they'd already come through the "big" battle.

Ree took a step toward the doorway, facing the room to block the guys off from leaving. Though she couldn't properly do that without putting her back to the tunnel, which would be asking for trouble. She settled for leaning against the wall by the door.

"Can't we find her with a tracking spell, you know, after we've had a chance to sleep and see a real doctor? Eastwood, you did this earlier with the ring. And if she's skipped town, we call up some friends and put together a posse. If she wants to run in the underground, someone will notice her.

Plus, Lucretia doesn't strike me as someone who'd be good at keeping a low profile."

Drake stepped in to her aid. "Ms. Reyes is correct—pursuing the witch now would be playing into her plans. We have wounded to tend to, and the proud, if bloodied, store to protect."

"Thank God, someone's making sense," Ree said.

Grognard cracked his neck, loud. "Yes it's dangerous, and I'm doing it. Eastwood and I have come through our share of tight scrapes just fine. You can stay here and mind the shop."

With that, Grognard grabbed his glaive-guisarme and walked out into the tunnel. Eastwood fetched a flare out of his jacket, along with a lanyard. He followed Grognard, cracking the glow stick as he went.

Ree face-palmed. "Clearly, we're in Bizarro World. So let's at least be smart about being ridiculous."

"Shall we join the light brigade or defend the fort?" Drake asked.

Ree turned to Joe. "Can you watch the others?" She fished around in her still-mucked pockets and pulled out a grimy key ring. It smelled like metallic ass. "You can even lock yourself in, because Grognard is a paranoid bastard. And if we aren't back by the time they get up, just hightail it."

Joe regarded the keys with a bit of fear, but he took them, nodded, and made his way to the office door, muttering to himself.

They could get lucky and find Lucretia all repentant and happy to go with them to her judgment. Ree could also win a lottery she never entered and be whisked away by Jennifer Lawrence to a life of luxury for no good reason.

She looked to Drake. "Theirs not to reason why." Then she set off through the door.

The inventor picked up his rifle and followed.

CHAPTER TEN

Dædalus, You Dick

Ree and Drake took the left-hand path away from Grognard's, following the older geeks' best bet at where to find Lucretia.

But as they turned the corner, someone or something hit a toggle on the universe.

Instead of a tunnel, the pair found themselves under a vast dome, with a starscape mural on the ceiling. The walls had opened up at the top, ending twelve feet up. Where there had been slowly cracking concrete and a base-running sluice for waste, the floor was now all cobbled stone, with small plants and tufts of grass peeking out through the sandy mortar here and there. And where the walls had been rough concrete, they were now finely layered brick. The air was crisper, a subtle breeze replacing the stale, musty air of the tunnel.

"The fuck?" Ree asked, turning in place. The corner behind her was gone, replaced by a solid wall. She stepped up and pushed on the stone, which was solid and cold and totally not there five seconds ago.

"My word," Drake said, turning as well. "This must be Lucretia's doing as well."

"But how?" Ree asked, prodding at the wall. She closed her eyes and walked forward slowly, wondering if there was some kind of perception filter, like she had to shut her eyes to move through the illusion.

Bonking her nose and the goggles against the brick put the lie to that idea pretty damn quick.

"Balls," Ree muttered. "Worth trying, though."

She turned to face the path before her. The air was open, so if they could go over the walls, life would be way easier.

"Why don't you bust out the aerothopter so we can take a look at what's up?" Ree suggested.

Drake nodded, setting his rifle against the wall and producing a folded-up brass-and-copper bundle. He set it on the ground before them and pushed a button. Ree backed up against the wall, in no particular mood to be smacked by a magically expanding pipe.

In fits and starts, the device unfolded and expanded, rocking from side to side as it wobbled its way to its full size. Totally expanded, the aerothopter was the odd lovechild of a Leonardo da Vinci design and a modern helicopter. It was all frame and engine, no fuselage, no weaponry, and no comfortable seating. And since Ree lacked natural posterior padding, it made the thing an incredibly uncomfortable ride. Not to mention the fact that she was still afraid of heights.

But they needed to catch up to Lucretia, or at least find a way out of wherever it was that they'd ended up.

"Are you sure you can't install some seating? I'd take cardboard, honestly," Ree said.

"I'm sorry, Ree, but I haven't found a way to add any material that close to the core without ruining the folding schema. It's rather like the Japanese tradition of origami, actually. Folds must be done in a certain order, to a certain degree, in order to preserve the integrity of the components and ensure the appropriate final shape."

Ree shrugged, climbing into what passed for the passenger seat.

"Well, if you get it figured out, I'll make it worth your while. I am happy to reward innovation with milk shakes and hero fries."

Drake made a typically masculine happy sound at the mention of the super-unhealthy delicacies. He may be a gentleman from an alternate Britain, but his palate had taken quite well to twenty-first-century American fare.

The inventor took the pilot's seat, and started the engine. Ree held the rifle, which was more secure than tying it to a crossbar. Plus, it gave her a chance to play a rails shooter if anything nasty showed up.

The vehicle lifted off, rotor blades less than a foot from each side of the walls.

"Keep it steady . . ." Ree said, her eyes glued on the walls. Running a rotor into the wall would go . . . poorly.

Drake pulled the aerothopter up and out of the hall, and Ree exhaled. They moved forward, and Ree took in the labyrinth below.

"Motherfrakker," she muttered as the immensity of the maze opened up around her. The winding paths of hallways unfolded in all directions for at least a hundred yards. Free of the tunneling effect of the halls, the whistle of the wind grew, pulling her hair free of her braid and whipping it across her face.

"Where the hell are they?" Ree asked, turning to look in all directions as she put her hair back in order.

"I will scale farther for a better view," Drake said, pulling the stick back and sending the aerothopter into a shallow climb. Their extreme lack of seat belts made steep climbs and dives "highly inadvisable," as Drake liked to say.

They were about eighty feet up when Ree caught a glimpse of Eastwood's green lightsaber near the far edge of the dome. "There!" she said, pointing across Drake's seat to a pathway far to their left.

Drake guided the aerothopter toward the light, and Ree continued to scan the maze, looking for Lucretia.

"Let me know if you see our Strega anywhere," she said, craning her neck around to look behind them.

Out of the corner of her eye, Ree saw something that looked neither like Lucretia nor her errant geeks. It looked like a fireball.

And it was coming right for them.

Ree shouted, "Fireball at eight o'clock!"

Drake banked left, diving to gain speed. The flaming sphere soared past to one side, missing the rotors by several feet.

Two more fireballs arced toward them from two directions, set ninety degrees apart.

"Nine and six!" Ree called, serving as Drake's rearview mirror.

Drake hauled back on the stick, pulling the aerothopter up out of the dive with the extra speed. They cleared one fireball, but the other detonated on the rotor. Ree leaned away from the explosion as licks of flame lashed out at the pair. The aerothopter rocked with the impact, and Ree wedged her feet between a set of pipes, holding on for gravity-defying life.

"Owfuckow!" Ree said, swatting at her burning hair with one hand.

The aerothopter went into an uncontrolled dive. Ree reached over and helped Drake haul back on the stick, even as the rotor groaned, one spoke white-hot as it melted toward the tip.

"Controlled crash?" she asked, her voice thin with panic.

Drake didn't respond, straining against the stick with all his strength as the maze came up to greet them with thick concrete slabs of lethal collision.

The world slowed as Ree ran the math on chances of pulling up in time, dying in a mangled wreck, and dying if they jumped.

Hoping she'd made the right call as the bottom of the aerothopter skipped off a maze wall, she pushed herself up and over and rolled sideways, grabbing Drake as she went. They fell out and down away from the aerothopter as it crashed.

She held on to Drake for dear life as they dropped to the floor, then remembered her training and went limp save for tucking her head. She had no chance to take the fall with a roll. It was all she could do to go ragdoll and pray that they'd survive.

Ree hit hard, bounced, then rolled along the floor, kicking up a plume of dust.

A hundred pains scrambled over one another for attention from her mind, overriding any chance for thought.

She focused on breathing. *In. Out.* But of course, her ribs and back hurt too, so even that kicked her ass.

But somewhere along the line, she managed to get her eyes open.

Drake was in a heap a few feet away, groaning in pain. *I hear you, man.*

She pulled herself into a ball, slowly, testing her injuries. Most everything hurt, but nothing felt broken. She might wake up dead the next day, but for now, it seemed like she could keep going.

"Drake?" she called.

The inventor coughed, spreading a plume of dust. "Present," he said, his voice a pained croak.

"Well, that blew chunks," Ree said, pulling herself up. A thin smoke trail pointed her toward the aerothopter wreck, and conveniently also served to orient her in the maze. Though as she remembered from the pulpy puzzle books she'd torn through as a kid, there was no guarantee that going vaguely forward and to the left would let them get where they wanted to be. She picked up Drake's rifle as she walked over to him. He pulled himself to a kneel, accepting Ree's offered hand.

She pulled him up, and they dusted themselves off. The ground was thick with sawdust, covered like the inside of a butcher's shop.

"Why the sawdust?" Ree asked to no one in particular, looking both ways. The sawdust ended in one way, but in the direction headed toward the elder geeks, it continued through the bend.

Drake bent to pick up a handful of the dust. He held it up and smelled it. "Beech, perhaps? Or cedar."

"I'm not sure how much that matters, but good to know," Ree said, trying to stretch the kink out. It hurt, but after a few stretches, she felt better.

"I was merely attempting to assemble some thoughts as to the disposition of the sawdust. There are a number of possibilities that come to mind, several of them fairly unsettling."

"Like we're in the labyrinth's butcher shop?" Ree asked.

"There is that. Also, the possibility that the labyrinth is under construction, and that there may be other beings present, perhaps even aside from those responsible for the fire blasts."

"Yep." They made their way toward the sawdust-y turn, moving as quietly as they could. Ree drew the jian, holding it in a low guard.

Ree peeked around the corner to see a one-room carpentry shop ahead. *That's not so bad, right?* Benches were stacked high with light-colored wooden planks, flanked by a collection of half-constructed benches, chairs, and chests. Beyond those, a finished cherry folding desk that looked like it belonged in Colonial Williamsburg.

"More wood," Ree said. Drake fiddled with his rifle, slotting a blue crystal in the chamber.

"Try this one the quiet way?" Ree asked. Drake nodded, and they hugged the wall of the passage, Ree in front, Drake over her shoulder, rifle at the ready.

They made it down most of the hall before someone crossed into view. The figure was about three feet tall, and wore a pair of faded denim overalls. He had a thick beard but short hair. He wore no shirt under the overalls, and was nearly as muscled as a romance cover model.

The muscular carpenter turned, and his eyes went wide as he saw Ree and Drake.

"More humans?" he said, sounding a little bit surprised and a little bit amused.

"More?" Ree asked as they walked into the room. "Who else has been here?"

The room was about thirty feet to a side, stocked with enough wood and machinery to fill a small warehouse with furniture. There were three workstations, but the burly little person was the only one around.

"Scruffy-looking guy in a coat and a rightly stout man with a polearm. They just passed through a few minutes back. Are you people using Spirit as a highway now, or what?"

Drake made the inhaling sound of realization at the same time as things clicked for Ree. *That would do it.* If they'd somehow crossed over into the Spirit realm through some subtle portal, that would actually explain a lot—why they'd been able to turn the corner and step from the sewer into a labyrinth, where all of those extra monsters had come from (Labyrinth, Minotaur, natch), and why there was a labyrinth in the first place.

"Can you tell us where they went?" Ree asked, skipping ahead to her objective. First, they had to find the other pair, then Lucretia, and then it was time to put this night to bed.

The small man (dwarf?) pointed behind him. "But you humans can't just wander through here like it's a bazaar. There's a reason I set up shop in a labyrinth. I don't like being disturbed, you hear? I like my peace and quiet."

Drake jumped in. Ree was happy to let him handle the diplomacy bits. "We're terribly sorry, sir. We are attempting to rejoin our companions and quit this place, so that we might leave you and this labyrinth to your business."

The small man nodded approvingly, stepping aside. "Get to it, then."

They hurried through the workshop and left the diminutive craftsman to his work.

"Seems like that guy doesn't get visitors very often," Ree said.

"I imagine that if one was used to going weeks without being interrupted, then to be so interrupted twice in a matter of minutes, would be quite disconcerting. I recall you acting not dissimilar when I called during one of your writing sessions," Drake said, wearing a knowing look he only got away with because of that smile.

"I was in the middle of the finale! It had taken me all week to figure out how to finish it up!

"But yeah, that's fair."

They reached a T-juncture. Ree looked both ways. One way had moss on the walls, ending with a turn to the left. The other had several halls branching off to each side.

"Where to, Captain Providence?" she asked.

Drake narrowed his eyes, evaluating each path. Then he stood with his eyes closed, breathing slowly.

Ree fidgeted, knowing that if she slowed down, she might not be able to get going again. She used to burn the wick at both ends plenty in college, but these all-nighters got a little harder every year.

Drake shook his head, then opened his eyes. "I feel nothing. If the universe is trying to guide me, I cannot hear it."

"Well, crap." Ree shrugged, walking down the hallway with the moss. "Lucretia is doing the most. I mean, overcompensation much?" Ree said, gesturing to the size of the room. "This is pretty elaborate revenge for losing out on an auction."

"I imagine the depth of her emotion stems directly from whatever it was that she planned to do with the ring," Drake said.

They reached the corner, and the maze bent around to the left, heading back in the direction Ree had dubbed "West" for the sake of clarity.

As she stepped to turn the corner, her foot sunk into the concrete, swallowing her to the waist.

Drake grabbed her under the arm and hit the ground hard behind her, stopping her descent. Her lower half started to burn, like her legs were all open wound and she'd just jumped into a pool of rubbing alcohol.

"Fuckity!" Ree said, pulling the sword out of the . . . *Ground? Acid? Whatever. Ow!*

Drake grunted, scrambling back. "What is this?" he said through gritted teeth.

Ree bit her tongue at the pain, then stumbled through the words as her tongue stung, joining the waaay-too-hopping pain party.

She pressed down on solid stone with her free hand. Engaging her core, she lifted her feet out of the liquid lie of a floor. Drake pulled her over and out, and she rolled across the ground, her legs smoking. She stood as fast as she could, intending to shake off the burning goop, only to discover that her pants had become as holey as Swiss cheese. Her sensible shoes looked like they'd been nuked in the microwave, and the breeze told her that the Swiss cheese properties extended all the way around her pants.

Because showing her ass in public was a great add-on to searing pain.

"Oh, my." Drake averted his eyes. Blushing, he'd gone red as a turnip. "Ms. Ree, I'm terribly sorry . . ."

"I know. Kind of naked-ish here," she said through gritted teeth, furious at what was either a gelatinous cube or just a random trap.

She removed her apron, turned it sideways, and tried to tie it into a miniskirt. No good. "Take this," Drake offered, handing her his coat. She wrapped it around the borrowed buff jacket, which didn't have nearly enough coverage for comfort. She belted the coat closed and looked back at the corner. The liquid floor rippled, covering just the 10 x 10 square of the corner, as best as she could tell. If they were lucky, they'd be able to jump the corner and keep going. But she wasn't about to jump into anything without testing the waters.

She pulled out one of the pens from her apron and lobbed it underhand. The pen clattered on the ground and rolled about a yard before stopping.

"Thank Jeebus," Ree said. "You good to jump that?"

Drake looked at the floor, and she saw the geometry wheels spinning behind his eyes. "Not a problem. But it may be best to mark this corner, lest we lose track and need to double back."

"Good thinking." Ree leaned down and ripped off a few inches of her shredded jeans, then tore the piece in half. She left one shred at their feet on the near side, then tossed the other around the corner.

"After you, m'lady," Drake said, matching an exaggerated gesture with a smile.

Ree sized up the corner again, then took several steps back. She pushed forward one, two steps, then pushed off on the third step, hiking up the coat-skirt as she did her best imitation of a long jumper, nearly clipping the inside corner as she went. She touched down without much grace, still running on fumes. She looked back to Drake, then mimicked his invitational bow.

She watched as Drake followed her lead, bounding around the corner with his rifle strapped across his back. As he set down, Ree heard fast footfalls behind her. But they weren't people feet.

Ree turned, raising the sword in front of her, and saw a centaur looking back at her. He was the old-school type— burly shirtless dude with sculpture-worthy muscles and a mane of hair that would make Fabio jealous. He held a bow drawn, arrow nocked. His hotness was mitigated by his murder-eyes.

"The hell?" she asked, accusing.

The centaur's gallop slowed. "Hades is far from here, mortal. This is the Labyrinth, and you are trespassing."

"Not on purpose." Ree waved her sword at his bow. "How's about you put that thing down before we have ourselves a fight scene?"

The centaur reeled back, whinnying. "It is you who are the trespasser. Lay down your arms and I may yet spare you."

Drake interjected, hands out in a classically reasonable display. "Noble sir, we mean no insult by our presence, for it was not our intent to come here. We mean only to reclaim our friends so that we might quit this place and leave you to your peace."

The centaur narrowed his eyes, settling back on all fours. "You are well-spoken for an outsider, young traveler. From where do you hail?"

Drake nodded. "Distant Avalon, good sir. I had the fortune to accompany the Contessa of the Lapis Galleon for several seasons, sailing the aetheric seas."

"The Contessa?" asked the centaur, enraged again. Dude must have a damned short temper. He raised his bow again. "That strumpet promised salvation to my cousins on the Straits of Haoron, but brought only destruction! You will pay for her crimes!"

"Mother. Fucker," Ree muttered, swinging at the centaur's bow as he drew back to fire at Drake. The Contessa had brought Ree more trouble than she could ever know, though she had to admit that if the wild-ass force of nature hadn't absconded with Drake, then Ree probably never would have met him.

Ree cut the head off of one arrow as she jumped to the side. The arrow spun off-target as it flew, shattering on the nearby wall. The centaur drew and fired again with incredible speed, but Drake dove to the side, rolling up to a crouch and drawing his rifle.

Meanwhile, Ree pressed, blade whirling. Equine Fabio had the high ground just by existing, and after his second shot, he used the bow to parry Ree's blade. The sword took chunks out of the wood, but not enough to stop the centaur from swinging at Ree with a powerful overhead strike. No way could she block that cut. Instead, Ree leaned to the side, deflecting the blow enough that it missed her entirely. But even deflecting the cut sent shock waves up her tired arms.

End this. Fast, she told herself. She sighed internally and swung low, hacking into the creature's thin foreleg.

Centaurs—wicked-strong, with most of the strengths of both horses and burly dudes. Also, the weaknesses of same. Her inner ten-year-old, who loved nothing in the world quite so much as horses (other than *Star Trek*, *Spider-Man*, and The New Kids on the Block), cried as she swung back at the centaur's rear leg. This time she hit above the hoof, cleaving deep. The centaur fell on its side, and she just barely dodged the creature's massive rump as it crashed to the labyrinth floor.

"I'm sorry about your cousin. But next time I see the Contessa, be sure I'll kick her ass for you."

The centaur flailed, acting more horse than man, looking like a wounded stallion about to be put down. Ree had no intention of being that person, and she hoped that the centaur could recover. For all she knew, the Contessa did destroy his cousins, but that wasn't her or Drake's fault. And they had places to be.

They hurried past the wounded centaur and rounded the corner.

⬩✕⬩⬡⬩✕⬩

At least half an hour later, they'd wandered, dead-ended, doubled back, and generally gotten themselves thoroughly labyrinthified.

Ree had no yarn, but Drake had chalk, so every time they made a turn, Drake marked the corner. This kept them from getting irrevocably lost but didn't help them find the older geeks.

Leaning against a wall as they took a break, Ree mused out loud. "I'd just yell for them, but chances are, all that'd do is bring us seven kinds of trouble from the locals, even if Grognard and Eastwood could hear us."

Drake nodded. "I fear you are correct. If we could locate the aerothopter, I might be able to repair it, but only if we were able to find a proper workshop."

"What about carpenter boy?" Ree asked.

"Wooden pieces would upset the weight balance, and I'm certain that at least one of the rotors will need to be replaced."

"Fucksticks," Ree said, more grumpy than actively pissed off. Lucretia was maxing out Ree's Hate Meter, leaving Wickham's rating in the dust. Pissing on her friend's achievements was bad, trying to get them killed was a whole other ball game, like the difference between croquet and *Blood Bowl*.

Ree leaned forward off the wall and cracked her neck. "Shall we?"

More twists, more turns. Three left turns later, instead of a dead end, they found themselves facing a long hallway straight out of *Tomb Raider*.

The walls had climbed to forty feet tall on both sides. In the hall proper, every other span of five feet (Ree couldn't help but think of them as squares in *D&D*, her life turned into a dungeon crawl) held a spike pit. A tall metal frame held bladed pendulums that swung in a tight pattern back and forth over the spike pits. And every third platform held an armored skeleton holding a pair of axes.

The skeletons raised their weapons in unison, their heads rattling on their spines like a boney cousin of the forest spirits from *Princess Mononoke*.

"Huh," Ree said. "That's new."

CHAPTER ELEVEN

Jump Jump Revolution

Ree watched the blades scythe back and forth for a few moments, trying to catch the pattern. Since the skeletons were just hanging out, she could assume that the platforms wouldn't sink under her like those hateful parts in platformer video games.

"Can you take care of the bone brigade?" Ree asked. Drake brought his rifle up and took aim.

The nearest skeleton crossed its axes, still rattling its head, now looking more like a baby toy for the kids of Metal-heads.

Drake fired. The blue blast ripped through the air, hitting the skeleton dead center. *Heh, dead.* But when the blue energy hit the axes, it dissipated into the weapon.

The axe glowed blue, and the skeleton pointed it back at Drake. In a totally unfair imitation of Link, the blast fired out from the axe, zipping past the swinging scythes.

Ree pushed Drake down and to the side, and the blast took a chunk out of the end of the hallway.

"Perhaps we should go another way," Drake said.

"Word," Ree said, getting back up. The pair backtracked, but when they tried to turn right, they were stopped by a dead end.

Ree tested the s that shouldn't be there with her sword, and it made the *tink* of hitting stone. Then she tested it with her open hand. It was cool, musty, and totally solid.

"Not fair!" Ree shouted, her mellow long since harshed. She pulled out her phone to check the charge: 12%. She'd turned on airplane mode when she established that the labyrinth didn't get cell signal, but even so, it didn't leave her with much oomph for magical power-ups.

"Thoughts?" she asked.

Drake tested the wall, gloved hand pressing against the stone. "I could attempt to remove the wall with an explosive, but there's no guarantee what little munitions I have on hand would be sufficient."

"You just carry explosives around on a regular basis?"

"Why shouldn't I? Your military uses grenades."

"But what about accidental explosions if you take a hit and land on something wrong?"

"That, my dear, is one of the advantages of using nontellurian physics. There is an element of volition required for my munitions. They're quite safe."

"What about exploding the skeletons, then?" she asked, turning back to the hall of death traps.

"I'm sure that my small devices would suffice, but it seems rather a waste. Bludgeoning attacks should suffice. The difficulty will be taking the occupied platforms."

Ree eyed the skeletons, which stood at attention, heads rattling. The nearest one's axe was back to normal, so Drake hadn't accidentally given it a permanent power-up.

"There're a few ways to do this. The *Prince of Persia* way, with swashbuckling, The *Tomb Raider* way, trying to climb up the rigging and brachiating our way over, and the *Doom* way, which would involve blowing everything up."

"I've always been partial to swashbuckling, but in this case, that would be quite bold."

"Quite," Ree said. The climb might be doable, but then

they'd still have to swing and jump to avoid the scythes.

Maybe there was an easier way. She pulled out her phone again, wishing she still had her sideboard or access to Grognard's to get her hands on some Turn Undead power. Again, she found herself wishing that there was a *D&D* movie worthy of fandom. There was the cartoon, but she couldn't honestly geek out over that anymore.

She pulled up a clip from *X2: X-Men United*, where Jean Grey threw around serious telekinetic power. She wouldn't need a big push, just enough to knock the skellies off their feet and into the pits. If she had more battery, she'd just go for some flight magic and hope that they could get over the wall without being fireballed to ashes.

"Can you keep an eye on the bone brigade for a minute?" Ree asked, starting the clip.

She heard Drake answer in the affirmative, but she was already zoning in on the scene, connecting with the character. Jean Grey, with her power growing inexplicably, driven by her devotion to the dream of her mentor, torn between the safety of Scott's familiar love and the excitement of the strange with Logan. The romantic anxiety angle hit home plenty well, even with her situation's differences from Jean's.

As the clip ended, Ree looked up to the skeletons and saw fire dancing at the edges of her vision. Several different minds whispered at the edge of her attention, but shut them out. She wouldn't get a lot out of the clip, and if she wasted any power, they might find themselves stuck in the middle of the hall while she tried to go back for a second dose.

"Ok, let's go," Ree said, stepping forward. The blades scythed back and forth, the skeletons waiting with axes shining and heads rattling.

She synced back up with the blades, watching the timing. "You good on these?"

"I've managed my fair share of deadly pits, thankfully," Drake said. "After you."

Ree winked at Drake, rocking back and forth. She found the timing, then jumped as the blade cut across the pit. Old-school platformers must have all been set in low-gravity worlds—Mario and Mega Man both had vertical leaps more than twice their height. She only needed five feet at a time, and thanked her "leadership" courses during junior high as she landed on the first stand-alone platform, staring across a second empty ledge at the skeleton beyond. She waited for the scythe in front, then jumped again, feeling the blade cut through the air behind her. *Eep.* That one was a shade faster than the other.

She heard Drake's soft grunt and turned to see him land on the first platform.

"And now," Ree said as she turned back to the skeleton. She reached out with one hand toward the skeleton, and put the other to her forehead, miming Jean Grey's most famous this-is-me-using-my-powers gesture.

And . . . push! She saw the skeleton topple over backward, crashing like a giant-size game of pick-up sticks.

Ree brought her hand down from her forehead and blew out the fake smoke on her not-gun finger. "Nice."

They bounded over several more pits, and Ree TKed the second skeleton as well.

But by the time she got to the platform in front of the third skeleton, the power was gone. Drake hopped beside her and she pulled out the phone again.

Ree pressed play on the video, and something overhead said, "Caaaaw!"

Ree snapped her neck up and around to see. A motorcy-cle-size crow arced over the labyrinth, then folded its wings into a dive, headed straight for them.

"Seriously?" Ree asked the universe, feeling cosmically shat upon. Drake popped off a shot, which blew a hole in the bird's wing, but it kept coming. It opened its wings, catching the air. The bird wavered, one wing's aerodynamicosity ruined by the smoldering hole, but managed to alight on the metallic frame holding the scythes, if ungracefully. It hopped from rung to rung.

"What would you say if I wanted to keep this one?" Ree asked.

"I'd say you're quite odd," Drake said, chuckling.

"Yeah. So what?"

Hopping down from the metallic frame, the corvid became a disturbing mashup of Edgar Allan Poe and *Super Mario Brothers*. Determined not to be squished like a Koopa, Ree sliced at the bird's foot, chopping off a toe. It unfurled its wings in the space between the scythes, wafting in the air.

Bad move, Bird-o. She spun the blade around for another cut, the weapon moving like flowing water in her hands. The jian wasn't a hefty weapon, but it handled like a dream. The slash took another chunk out of the creature, and it cawed at ninety decibels right in her face. It followed up with a peck, which she dodged by ducking to a squat, thankful for her young knees. She swung again, and got a splatter of ichor for her trouble.

Drake had dropped his rifle and pulled out his kukri, waving it in a distracting defensive pattern. There wasn't room for two humans, a monster, a sword, and a rifle all in the same square, so he'd decided to fight smart, letting her handle the melee portion of the encounter.

She stood with a thrust, burying the blade deep in the creature. It dropped like an anvil, straight on top of her and Drake. The three hit the platform, then rolled off. Ree kept her chest on the plaftorm, holding on with her free arm, thankful for the rough texture of the surface, which gave her half-decent handholds. She felt her back pop when Drake stopped himself by grabbing her around the waist. The bird slid off her sword to fall and impale itself on the spike pit, so at least she wasn't holding up two whole other entities.

Mothergodddamnedfuckingow.

"Climbing would be good, thanks!" Ree gasped out, her fingers already shaking. At least she was wearing the thick leather coat, not him. That ten pounds distributed on her frame was a lot better than tugging at her hips.

She heard frustrated clambering, and tried to not take it personally as Drake grabbed his way up her body to pull himself onto the platform. What would have been terribly intimate touching in another context was just thoroughly uncomfortable and lung-crushing in this one, so it was easier to file it all away under "Not contributing to the life-as-CW-drama."

Gloved hands wrapped around her arms, and Ree pulled herself up, with Drake's help, leaving the pair to hyperventilate on the platform. Nearby, the skeleton rattled like a puppy whining for attention.

"Take a number," Ree gasped, waving lazily with one hand.

They took a minute to catch their breath. Her lungs were bellows, sucking in air as hard as she could to remind her lungs that oxygen was a good thing. Ree sat up and looked at the eager skeleton. "How long have you been waiting to fight somebody?" she asked out loud. Grognard and Eastwood couldn't have come this way, unless they'd evaded the skeletons (or they re-spawned). But since she couldn't go back anyway, the only way out was through.

"You know what?" Ree said. "I'm done with this shit. It's time to cheat."

Drake raised an eyebrow but said nothing. She had a good rar on, and it was just as well that he not feed it by being reasonable when she was trying to rage.

Another trip to Jean Grey Lane gave her the magic to send the last skeleton flying, and they huffed their way across the pits to the end of the hall, where the walls dropped back to just over ten feet high.

"And now, we start getting sneaky," Ree said. She called up *Spider-Man* on her phone and watched the first wall-crawling clip, her battery ticking down from 3%.

"We're going up and then we're going to roof-run our way through this maze until we find the guys, then we're going to GTFO so I can go to bed. Sound good?"

"Certainly," Drake said.

Ree felt the Spider-magic tingling softly in her brain. She had to get up and get Drake up in one go, since her phone didn't have the juice for more than that. *Let's just hope it's enough.*

"I'll go up, then I'm going to pull you up with the rifle. I don't have long, so chop chop." Ree jumped at the wall and stuck with her hands and feet. She pulled herself up the wall, the increased strength making the task way easier than her last climb. She reached the top of the wall and reached back. Drake held up the rifle, and she grabbed it, pulling as he walked his way up the wall.

She pulled herself up onto the top of the stone as she felt the Spider-magic fading, and straddled the two-foot-wide wall as she helped Drake reach the top. *Don't look down*, she told herself. Looking down would give fuel to that part of her brain that housed her fear of heights.

And that wouldn't end poorly at all.

Ree sat up and saw the maze from above, looking out instead of down. She couldn't see into more than a couple of rows on either side before the shallow horizon cut her off, but from a standing position, they'd be able to avoid the traps, and would hopefully be low enough to dodge whatever was sending the fireballs. They just had to avoid falling and cracking their skulls open if anything nasty did decide to come and get them while they were doing their Parkour act.

She got to her feet with the last of the *Spider-Man* power, then took a long breath as she steadied herself. There was no wind in the labyrinth, which was a rare blessing from the universe that she felt was otherwise hating her. Ree scanned around, looking for the green light of a lightsaber or the swishy crinoline of one of Lucretia's voluminous dresses.

Don't look down fought with *You have to look down, dork*, and she took several deep breaths before she let her gaze drift toward the labyrinth floor.

Off to one side stood a Dungeonpunk American Gladiators obstacle course in wood, concrete, and water, a steep ramp down into a dark pit sort of area lit only by glowing blue eyes, and to one side, a set of catapults crewed by scaly green creatures with pointed ears that stuck straight out from their skulls.

"You got anything?" she asked, looking around.

"I'd suggest avoiding those catapults," he said. Ree nodded to that. "The fireballs came from there," he said, pointing again, "so I recommend we head this way. If we can find the aerothopter, I may be able to jury-rig it enough to fold up so that I can carry it away for later repair."

"In that case, we go this way, right?" Ree said. Taking the high road would invalidate their chalk-based trail marking pretty damned fast.

They made their way along the narrow wall. Ree held the sword out for balance, and Drake used his rifle as a tightrope walker's pole. They passed monsters, pits, and dead ends, and with every step, Ree felt better about taking the high road.

Several minutes later, they found the smoldering wreck of the aerothopter. It was not alone.

A pack of blue-skinned creatures with forked tails poked at the crashed contraption. They looked like Bamfs from *X-Men*, Nightcrawler-esque creatures the size of four-year-olds.

"That's probably not good," Ree said.

"Most certainly not. Those don't appear to be gremlins, but there is no shortage of creatures able to ruin an already-damaged device."

The hallway with the aerothopter wasn't accessible on their wall, so they had to drop down and wind around several corners.

By the time they'd arrived, the creatures had grown in number, and the aerothopter was in even worse shape. *That's not encouraging,* Ree admitted. Were these creatures born out of destruction or something? Gremlins that created and fed on atrophy? *That would blow chunks, and they need to stay very far away from my apartment. Place is enough of a pig's sty as is.*

"Melee to avoid damaging your poor contraption any more than necessary?" Ree asked, raising her sword.

"That would be preferable, yes."

Ree strode forward, whipping her sword around and trying to make as much noise as possible. If these things were scavengers, maybe they were also cowards. She'd had her fill of fighting. Just moving was effort enough. Fatigue clawed at her eyes like sandpaper, and her limbs felt like lead.

Stay on target. . . .

One of the creatures hissed at Ree, its eyes glowing red, but its companions broke and ran, screeching as they padded away on all fours. The angry one saw that it was alone, and as Ree closed to stab at it, it jumped onto the unbroken rotor and swung itself up to the top of the wall, bounding over and out of sight.

"I'll take fights like that for the rest of the night, thank you very much," Ree said, sheathing the sword as she stepped up to the aerothopter.

It was still recognizable, which was a plus. But one rotor was broken, and nearly everything about the vehicle was folded, spindled, or mutilated.

"So, Doc, what's the diagnosis?" she asked as Drake regarded the wreck.

Drake took several long breaths, his nostrils flaring. Drake was a pretty chill guy, even with all the swashbuckling excitement. He was several degrees more unflappable than Ree, putting him very close to the Helen Mirren side of the flappability continuum (the other side being eternally put-upon comic heroine Cathy, natch).

He knelt down and fiddled with buttons, levers, and something that Ree still couldn't label anything other than *whatsit*. He poked and prodded, but nothing moved.

With another sigh, Drake stood. "It's impossible. I cannot fix the aerothopter, not even enough for it to collapse."

"But you can build another one, right? With enough time?"

Drake grabbed a pipe of the machine, holding on like he was in a boat tossed upon rough waters. "I made this during my tenure on the Lapis Galleon, using alloys found only in the deepest reaches of the aetheric sea. Barring another expedition into the outer reaches of Faerie, I fear that you may never again have the misfortune of squeezing determinedly into a Drake Winters aerothopter."

Sympathetic grief on behalf of Drake outweighed a tiny bit of relief. Without that aerothopter, we might not ever have caught the Aberrant Muse, and I'd have had a hell of a lot worse time getting away from Rachel MacKenzie. And however useful it was, it was important to him, something he was proud of.

Ree put a hand on Drake's shoulder and squeezed. She didn't dare doing anything more, as punch-drunk blood loss and exhaustion had made her filters pretty thin, and that way lay self-destruction and hurt feelings.

"We'll get you the parts. Can you salvage anything?"

Drake said, "There's a screwdriver in the coat. Third pocket from the left. Would you be so kind?"

Ree straightened up. She hadn't felt a screwdriver in the coat . . . She reached inside the heavy coat and felt around. Lo and behold, a screwdriver.

"Huh," she said, handing it to Drake. The world of magic never failed to amaze.

The inventor crouched down and fiddled with the ruined aerothopter. Ree kept an eye out for the Bamf-esques or anything else that might be wandering around.

"So how do we take out Lucretia if we find her before the others?" Ree asked as Drake worked.

"Overwhelming force, I rather imagine. Her Hexomancy can do only so much. Thus far, I've only seen her efforts directed at one individual at a time, or at an environment, with very specific effects, as seen in Grognard's. I believe that if both of us were to attack at once, we'd be able to overcome her powers. And if we had all four assembled at the same time, it should be all the easier."

"Just as long as the magic she uses to fuck with one of us doesn't screw over the others. Friendly fire isn't."

Ree heard wind whistling along the hallway to the west, and she narrowed her eyes, one hand going to the goggles, wishing she knew how to change the filters.

"You got an infrared mode on this set?" she asked.

Drake stopped, then counted fingers on his left hand. "Third wheel from the back, on the left. Two clicks clockwise."

Ree adjusted the wheel, and then her vision switched into *Predator* mode. The walls were cool blues and greens. She scanned through the hall, passing over Drake's orange, red, and white form. The still-smoking aerothopter showed in cool oranges and yellows.

As she looked back to the far end of the hall, a blotch of white and red passed out of sight, bearing north.

"Drake, did you see that?"

"Alas, no. Should I be worried?"

"Something just passed that way. How's it going here?"

Drake grunted as he stood up. "The only things worth salvaging can't be salvaged. So for a memento, I have this." She saw a hunk of cooling blue-green. She lifted the goggles to see a single lever, one that he used for pitch. Or yaw. She forgot.

"That blows," Ree said, offering a sympathetic look.

She waited for a minute while Drake gathered his composure. She thought about how much he'd risked and sacrificed for her. If he did this much for his friends, she could only imagine how much he'd done for Priya.

"Let's go check out who that was." She dropped the goggles back into place, and started hustling down the corridor.

She stopped at the corner, looked in the direction the figure had come from, then peeked her head around the corner. Thankfully, this was a long hall, so she just caught the same figure duck around another corner.

"Follow me!" Ree said, setting off at a jog.

Steady bootfalls told her Drake was with her. She leveled her gaze to keep both floor and the end of the hall in view, just in case the mysterious whomever decided to double back.

"They turned there," Ree said, gesturing with the sword.

"Understood. Could it be Lucretia?"

"Maybe. These don't get great resolution at fifty feet."

"My apologies. As a reserve set, they were lower on my schedule for upgrades and calibration."

"I'm not griping, just saying. I'm a little bit totally exhausted. Sorry if I'm coming off snippy." *Not that you're ever snippy at your best,* a self-effacing voice said in her mind. *Shush,* she told herself.

They reached the end of the hall, and Ree peeked around the corner to see stairs leading down into a muddy pit of still water. Steps climbed back out of the water twenty feet later, but who knew how deep the pool was, or what sorts of nastiness might call that muck home?

And on the other side stood the figure, holding a long, cool cylinder.

"You see that?" Ree asked.

"See wha—" Drake was cut off as a shot rang out.

Drake collapsed. Ree dove down to cover him as another shot filled the hall. She heard an impact against the far wall, and when she looked up, the same heat signature vanished behind the cool blue of the wall.

"Fuckinggoddamnedhells," she said, pulling the goggles off to look at Drake.

Where was he hit? she asked herself, looking over the inventor. There were no red patches on his white shirt, or his pants.

She leaned in, in case her crap eyesight was making her miss the obvious. After a Taking 20 amount of time, she still couldn't see an entry wound. But Drake was out cold. She took his pulse. Subdued, but alive.

"The fuck is this?" she asked out loud. *Did invisi-person have a tranquilizer blow dart? Blaster set to stun?* She tried to inventory the weapons with a stun power from the store, and quit after seven. *Too many variables. Need more data.* "Drake? C'mon, dude, get up." She poked and prodded, jostled and shoved, then tugged on the unconscious inventor, trying to get him to sit up. Nothing worked, and trying to keep him upright was about as easy as getting a bag of lumpy potatoes to sit upright.

Ree grumbled as she set Drake down gently, trying to keep from adding blunt head trauma to his list of injuries. She wasn't about to leave him alone with a jillion and one neighborhood monsters.

"Sorry in advance," Ree said, then leaned in and shouted, "DRAKE!"

Nothing.

Ree devolved into mutter-cursing as she grabbed Drake under his arms. She turned him around and started dragging the inventor down the hall. She wouldn't get very far like this—not fast, anyway. And if whoever had done this wanted to get away, now they would. But them's the breaks. Lots of breaks. Bad breaks, worse breaks, and oh-God-I'm-going-to-be-sore-tomorrow breaks.

But since complaining had yet to make anything in her life better outside of that one time shaming an airline on Twitter, she soldiered on.

I am getting so many milk shakes when this is all done.

CHAPTER TWELVE

The Battle of the Six Egos

Ree lost track of time as she dragged Drake through the maze. She stopped every so often to wheeze, prod Drake with the hope that he'd wake up and relieve her of the dragony, then give up and start moving again.

The infrared filter on the goggles revealed nothing, but Ree bet that as soon as she turned the filter off, something invisible would drop-kick her, steal her beer money, and scurry off to gloat.

I deserve a raise. That thought would have sustained her, save for the fact that Grognard's business was probably hosed. But she did *deserve* the raise, and that was something.

She rounded another corner, going back to using Drake's chalk to mark their journey. The piece splintered a bit more each time she marked a turn, and the diminishing nub was approaching powder. Not that she actually knew where they were in the labyrinth anymore.

Halfway down the hall, she took another break to look around a T-juncture that split off to the east.

Revealing a squadron of less-cool-than-their-surroundings humanoid shapes goose-stepping toward her, two by two.

She pulled off her goggles again to see ranks of Bronze-Age-y toy soldiers advancing on her position, each holding a spear. They were each about two feet tall. At ten rows, two by two, that made for twenty possible problems inbound.

"Charge!" came a high, tinny voice. The figure's sword raised in challenge.

So. Many. Milk shakes, Ree thought to herself, running back to haul Drake to the far side of the T-juncture. That way, if she needed to beat a retreat, she wouldn't have to go back through the tin men to get to him.

She set Drake down so that she could start dragging with the least delay, then poked the inventor one time in the chest, then cheek.

"Drake? It'd be really great if you could wake up now."

Still nothing.

"Once more unto the breach, dear . . . me," Ree said, feeling the exhaustion even more. She stood several feet back from the corner so she could see the toys as they approached and take cover. Sadly, as a righty, she'd be cutting off her range of motion, with her right shoulder against the wall. That meant she'd have to stick and move, all the more important with that many opponents. With luck, they'd all be minion-y, and she could mow through them in a hurry.

The first soldier came into view, and she took it off at the head with a flicking cut from the wrist. She cut at its neighbor with a back-edge cut, but that one got its shield up in time. Instead, her blow just knocked it off its feet and across the floor. Ree stepped to her left and cut back, trying to catch the second row. But the next pair of soldiers had their shields up.

She danced with them for a minute, giving ground sparingly and trying to keep the soldiers on the defensive. She had reach and strength on her side, but 19–1 were pretty grim odds.

She fought cut by cut, kick by kick, and even threw in a bit of wrestling that made her feel vaguely Gulliver-esque. In a minute or so, she stood surrounded by a field of broken toys and scattered blades, only a couple bruises and minor cuts worse for the wear.

"I'd really like to go home now," Ree said, cracking her neck again as she moved to pick up Drake and resume the dragging drudgery.

She rounded the corner to the sound of distant voices. Ree slowed, trying to drag as softly as possible. As she got closer, the voices became a bit more distinct. They were higher-pitched, one in the alto register, the other a clear soprano.

But what are they saying? Ree stopped to listen, closing her eyes and focusing on the words.

". . . them here. I said him, and only him," said one voice, the alto.

"You said lead them out, I led them. I activated the charm, and then I opened the gate. I did my part. Now pay up."

"Not until he is delivered to me."

A gasp of exasperation. "Bringing them here was your idea, and now you want me to go play fetch? Double."

"You'll bring him, or you get nothing, and you can find your way out of here on your own."

Unless the labyrinth had voice-changing powers, or doppelgängers, then the alto was Lucretia. And the soprano was Wickham.

"Gorram Toaster-loving ass," Ree whispered, setting Drake down. The Lieutenant might be mostly a pushover, but even having an extra body in the way would make fighting Lucretia harder. And as she'd said with Drake, just throwing one person at a time at Lucretia was a recipe for failsauce.

"Drake, I really need you to wake up, okay? We need to kick Wickham's ass. You hear that? Leftenant Arrogance needs a smackdown."

Surprisingly, Drake's eyes fluttered. He shifted in her grip, stretching like someone coming out of a deep sleep. She was usually the late sleeper in her relationships, but she'd been the first up a number of times, especially on Fuck Insomnia™ nights.

"What now?" he asked sleepily.

Ree responded in a whisper. "Keep it down. We're close."

Drake blinked open his eyes and stared at Ree, his eyes bloodshot. "Ms. Ree? Close to what?"

"Wickham and Lucretia. Wickham sold us out, from the sound of it. No sign of the boys just yet. You good for a fight?" Ree offered the rifle, as if the weapon would help him shake off the stun.

Drake took the weapon and used the stock to help him push up to his feet. A couple of wobbles later, he was upright.

"I believe so, but I may need a moment to gather my sorts."

"Don't wait too long. Who knows when they might leave?"

Drake took a long breath, then straightened himself. "So be it. Lead on, Ms. Ree."

Ree crept forward, sword at the ready. She reached the corner, then arranged her goggles so that she could see the invisible Wickham.

She leaned around the corner centimeter by centimeter until she saw the edge of a black crinoline dress. Leaning back, Ree whispered, "Lucretia's closer to us, we take her first. Keep them pinned as I go in, then fire on Wickham. If we're lucky, Lucretia's as beat as we are. And I think my cardio is better than hers."

"It's undisputable that you have a finer heart than the fate witch."

"True, but not what I was say—" Ree shook her head. "Never mind. Thanks. Let's go."

Ree raised her sword, dug into the jacket for the screw-driver, and then dove around the corner.

Lucretia and Wickham were there, and the world slowed as Ree charged, sword held forward like a lance. A saner voice in her head reminded the rest of her that she should probably start carrying a sturdier bludgeoning weapon for times like this, where a supreme ass-kicking was called for, but homicide was off the table.

Gorram Chaotic Good aversion to actually killing people. Lucretia flicked her wrist, and Ree tripped over her own feet. Expecting something ridiculous like this, she dove forward into a shoulder roll, recovering forward and pushing back to her feet.

Several bolts zipped over her shoulder, forcing the two women to break apart. Wickham reached for her blaster while Lucretia produced a misericord stiletto from the folds of her dress.

Twenty feet left. Ree pushed forward, a roar building in her throat and leaping out into the cool air of the labyrinth.

As she prepared to lunge at Lucretia, a stone slid out from underfoot, sending her sprawling again. She steadied herself on the ground, then threw the screwdriver to distract the fate witch.

Throwing an empty gun at Superman might do nothing, but chucking a foot of steel at Lucretia at least got the woman to duck. And while ducking, there was no cursing.

Ree advanced again and cut at the woman's limbs, trying to push her into the back of the alcove they'd been using for their conversation, a 10 x 10 space carved into an otherwise straight hallway.

More blasts hit the opposite wall, keeping Wickham on the ropes.

Ree brought the sword around to go for a non-fatal wound, and the sword leapt out of her hands, clattering to the floor.

"So be it," Ree said, diving forward in a Bull's Rush. She may not have the applicable feats, but she trusted her hundreds of hours of knife defenses. And out of anyone in the Pearson Underground, she was stronger than Lucretia.

The two of them slammed into the wall. Ree grabbed Lucretia's hand, holding the misericord away from either of them. The thing was like a baby rapier, and would quite handily pierce deep into any organ, anywhere, were it allowed. It wasn't.

Lucretia fought back with surprising ferocity.

"Graceless harpy! You will pay too! That ring was my last chance, you absolute muppet! Do you know what you've wrought?"

What? Ree asked. She'd been expecting villain banter, but not You've-doomed-us-all! rhetoric.

It had to be a trick. A weird one, but whatever. *I don't have time for this shit.*

"I have no fucking clue," Ree said as the women wrestled, toppling to the ground, "what you're talking about. And I don't care." Ree maneuvered her way to the side, and then atop Lucretia, years of Hapkido letting her flow from the mount to side-control, to her own mount, straddling the woman with her legs and witch woman's core with her hips. She didn't have as much body weight, which meant she'd had to learn exactly where to put herself to make it count. And at least this time, she had Drake's coat helping out.

It helped again as Lucretia muttered something in Japanese. Ree's grip on the woman's wrist slipped. She slammed her hand forward, jamming the misericord through the jacket. The coat took a lot of the hit, more than she was expecting. It was magicked too, like the shambles of the buff coat below it. Even with two armored layers, the blade still punched straight through her left shoulder. The one where she'd been shot just a month before.

"FucknuggetmuncherOW!" Ree screamed, pain dropping her on her back.

Ree heard boots on stone as she struggled to keep Lucretia from stabbing again. Both hands pushed back on Lucretia's arm. Ree threw a kick, trying to hit groin, hip, thigh, anything. She needed space and time to get her equilibrium and let skill come back into play.

"Little help, please?" Ree croaked, lashing out with kick after kick. Now-bare shins hit steel-boned corsetry and Ree wasn't sure who was taking more damage. *Don't care, keep going.*

Ree took a kick to the side from an impossible angle. Had to be Wickham.

And a split second later came the *whack!* of wood against bone.

Lucretia's focus flitted away, and Ree seized the opportunity, turning the woman's wrist inward and stripping the dagger from her grip, her shoulder screaming pained epithets all the while.

And for my next trick . . . Ree wrapped her arms around Lucretia's just above the elbow, forcing the woman's arms into hyper-extension.

"Got you!" Ree said, and slammed the pair into the ground, side by side. No hand gestures, no magic. Ree flexed the hold, and Lucretia screamed. It sounded like a good idea, so Ree joined her.

Shooting pain forced Ree to release the hold. Instead, she gave the fate witch one more cross to the face, then disentangled herself, her vision wavering.

"Medic?" Ree asked, feeling four kinds of not okay. Nausea, blood loss, exhaustion, blunt force trauma, her problems piled up like a Jay Z song.

Got 99 problems and a witch is one.

Hands wrapped around her, and she leaned into Drake, then moved the pair to the wall. She leaned against the cool stone and looked at the scene.

Lucretia was out. Wickham was disarmed, her arms tied in front of her. Drake had the beginnings of what would be an epic shiner but didn't seem to have collected any other new injuries.

"You know how to get out of here?" Ree asked in Wickham's direction. The world still wavered, unconsciousness go-go dancing at the edges of her vision.

Not yet, girlie. Gotta get the hell out, first.

"No. You managed to KO the only person here who can get us out."

"If she made this whole place, shouldn't it have gone poof when she dropped off?" Ree asked.

Wickham rolled her eyes. "You think Lucretia could make all of this? What she made was a portal, linking the sewer to a particular isolation pocket of the Spirit realm, but only she can take us back. That is, unless you're actually not entirely useless and can do it yourself."

Ree said, "Sally Strega will be back around in a few. It's not like I stunned her with a blaster or anything."

Wickham winced at that, proving her hunch. Wickham was a model, not an actress. Her nervous behavior earlier made a hell of a lot more sense now. She'd been sitting around for hours leading up to her low-rent Judas act, rubbing elbows with the very people she was about to screw over. The fact that she'd been uncomfortable actually spoke to inklings of humanity.

"How much was she going to pay you?" Ree asked.

"Enough."

"What happened to the trust fund? The platinum card?"

"High-risk investment portfolios. When they win, they win big. And when they lose . . ."

Drake bit back a comment. *I got this,* Ree thought, squeezing his arm.

"So you sold us all out because you fucked up on the stock market? You were willing to kill a half-dozen people just to finance your hand-picked version of Steampunk?" Ree asked.

"I've already made my opinions on your pathetic clubhouse known," Wickham said. "The fact that you didn't figure it out only shows how moronic you all are."

Ree cracked her knuckles. "So what's stopping me from roughing you up something fierce, Ms. Part-Time-Model?"

"Your infantile sense of morality, I'd wager. You don't have the conviction to kill me, which is what you should do."

"Maybe I don't, but my friend Eastwood's been flirting with the Dark Side these days. Maybe I should just hand you over to him."

That got a reaction. Wickham's eyes widened.

Let that sink in a while, Ree thought.

Wickham's silence was answer enough.

"Do you know where Eastwood and Grognard are?" Drake asked.

"Somewhere off that way," Wickham said, pointing southeast.

"How far?" Ree asked.

"Far enough to not hear the fight, apparently."

Fuck it.

"BOSS!" Ree shouted, aiming her voice upward. Let the monsters come. She was not going to spend the rest of the night wandering around a fucking death trap while her boss and Eastwood also wandered around said fucking death trap, their paths crisscrossing like a *Scooby-Doo* skit.

No answer. She turned in the other direction and cupped a hand to her cheek. "BOSS!" "EASTWOOD!" Her shouts dissipated into the vast dome above the labyrinth. "Any ideas?" Ree asked, turning to Drake.

"We could climb the walls once more and try to gain a higher vantage point."

Ree checked her phone. It turned on long enough to laugh at her and then go back to sleep.

"Fresh out of juice. You think you can boost me up far enough?" Ree said, nodding at the twelve-foot-tall walls that enclosed the hallway.

Drake regarded the wall. "I think not." And anyway, they couldn't take to the walls entirely, since they'd have to haul Lucretia around and keep an eye on Wickham.

Ree wandered around for a few minutes while Drake kept tabs on the Violently inclined Femmes.

Zip. Zilch. Nada. Bupkes. And other crappy nothings.

She was about to double back to go the other way when she heard soft footsteps, coming fast. They got louder, closer, and Ree looked down a hall to see Eastwood and Grognard round the corner. They were sucking wind, but moving at an impressive clip, especially considering the weight Grognard was hauling around with that chain shirt. But Ree had learned that fairly amazing things were possible with the power of adrenaline. And who knows, maybe Eastwood'd had his own sideboard.

Her thoughts were derailed when she saw fireballs with eyes and gaping maws follow them around the corner, crackling like beach-ball-size bonfires.

One of the three crashed into the wall, obliterating the stone. But the other two made the corner, just a dozen paces behind the sweat-drenched geeks.

"Run!" Grognard yelled, waving Ree off.

"What the hell?" Ree asked, as much about their absence as the flaming Pac-Man-alikes following them.

"I said run!" Grognard said again. Eastwood looked up and waved her off as well.

She spun on her heels and headed down the hallway back toward Drake and company.

"Fireballs incoming!" she said. "Grab Lucretia!" The woman might be a sadistic bitch, but Grognard wouldn't get any cash out of her to fix the store if they left her to die.

"Did you say fireballs?" Wickham asked, her eyes wide even from fifty feet out.

"Motherfucking fireballs! As in run away from them!" Ree said, her lungs, legs, and abdomen burning.

Wickham took off down the hall as Drake tossed Lucretia over his shoulder in a fireman's carry, her voluminous skirts obscuring his vision.

"This will prove problematic," he said, trying to adjust the woman to give himself a view.

Running was one thing, but if they couldn't outmaneuver the fireballs, then someone would fall behind until they became barbeque.

"Drake, you got any ice crystals left?"

The inventor froze, then straightened. "Third rear pocket,

the fold with two snaps!" Drake fumbled around until he un-slung his rifle.

Eastwood and Grognard rounded the corner.

"What are you doing? Run!" Grognard said, wheezing.

"I got this, boss!" Ree said, stopping to grope around in Drake's jacket.

One, two, three. The pouch she found had one strap, so she reached around the area.

Three there, another one.

Ah, there we are!

She unsnapped the fold and breathed in so she could reach down into the pocket. Her fingers closed around a cold, smooth cylinder, and she pulled out a glowing ice-blue crystal.

"Eureka!" she said, accepting the rifle from Drake. She pulled the locking whatever thing back and dumped the current crystal out as Grognard said, "Clear the hall!" Ree leaned against the wall as she loaded the crystal into the rifle.

Come on, come on. No time to be tired, no time to be slow.

She raised the rifle and fired. The blast clipped the nearest fireball, freezing it over the course of a second like Cryo Ammo in *Mass Effect*. The sphere dropped to the floor like a bowling ball and shattered.

Grognard passed the group, leaving just Eastwood and a fireball hot (yes, hot) on his heels.

"Duck! Dive! Something!" Ree said.

"It's too close! Toss me the rifle!" Eastwood said, hobbling forward with a limp.

"Are you kidding?!"

"Goddamnit, trust me!" Eastwood said with desperation in his voice.

Time slowed as she thought back to their fight that had kicked off the night, about holding the door together, fighting back to back.

He'd keep fucking up. Everyone fucked up. He was totally emotionally compromised about her mom, even more than she was. But he always came through in the end.

Ree tossed the rifle to Eastwood and slammed herself back at the wall.

Eastwood caught the rifle, and in one smooth motion, he lifted it over his head and fired without aiming.

The fireball started to freeze, then shattered as it exploded against Eastwood's back, knocking the man to the floor.

Holy crap.

From behind her, Lucretia shouted, "Yes!"

Ree looked over to see the fate witch looking over Drake's shoulder, far less unconscious than she'd looked just five seconds before. *Sneaky git.*

But she hadn't gotten him. Right?

Ree pushed off the wall and knelt down next to her one-time mentor. "You okay?"

The man was still for a moment. Then he gasped, taking in a large breath.

Eastwood uttered a string of curses, his lungs bellowing with visible effort. "I'm getting too old for this stuff."

"I'll take that as a yes?" Ree said, her heart ten pounds lighter.

"It'll have to do for now," the man said, pushing himself up to his feet.

Ree turned back to Grognard. "Are you okay?"

The bartender wheezed, clearly pained. "Just a couple cracked ribs. I'll be fine."

"Where's Wickham?" Drake asked, spinning in place. He'd dropped Lucretia to the floor. The woman backed herself up to the wall, and started doing something with her hands.

"No." Grognard took one big step over to the fate witch and dropped her to the ground with a fluid motion that spoke of years of work being his own bouncer. The moving stopped.

But Wickham was gone. "If I weren't so pissed off, I'd be impressed. Twice in one night," Ree said.

Eastwood walked over to Lucretia and knelt down, speaking into her ear.

"You're going to answer for all of this. I hope you've got a fortune squirreled away somewhere, because by Grognard's estimate, you owe him half a million in damages."

Lucretia spat at Eastwood. "The only thing I owe is retribution. When you were traipsing around trying to bring your dead girlfriend back, I was trying to correct the course of history. And now it's nearly too late. If you have any sense, you'll release me at once and join my quest."

"The fuck are you talking about?" Ree said. *Self-important much?*

"Perhaps we should adjourn from the maze full of death traps to discuss this further," Drake said as something tenebrous winged its way across the sky.

Lucretia sighed. "If someone would kindly remove his massive knee from the small of my back, I would happily lead us all out of here so we can have a reasonable discussion like adults."

Grognard released the pressure and pulled Lucretia to her feet, hands locked behind her back. "No cutesy shit, got it?"

"Understood," Lucretia sneered.

They took Lucretia on a winding perp walk, the fate witch directing them through turns until they came to a dead end. She opened a portal, one hand always restrained by Ree or Grognard. But finally, after what felt like a week in the *verdampt* place, they made their way back into the sewer, and to Grognard's.

Shade had come to, so when they returned, Talon and Chandra pledged to walk the battered cyberpunk home. The group made their farewells, most failing to hold back their dagger-eyes for Lucretia, the architect of their ruined night.

When the others had gone, Lucretia asked for a glass of water, and then began.

"What you have to understand is that everything has already gone wrong. And there isn't much time left to set things right."

Timekeeper

Lucretia spoke matter-of-factly, with none of the drama that often went into her speech.

"If time is a river, then I am a custodian, making certain that when a tree falls into the stream, it is removed, so that the flow is not disturbed. My sisters and I monitor the strands of fate and probability to anticipate disturbances and to ensure that history flows as it ought, directed by human action."

Ree raised a hand. "Holdonasec. Why have I never heard about this before? Normally you're all Scheming Vengeance Lady, now all of a sudden you're supposed to be some Rorikon Time Cop?"

Lucretia took a long drink, her eyes never leaving Ree. "My business is my own, child. And my sisterhood finds that we can do our duty best when we don't advertise ourselves. But since Mr. Eastwood has so blithely disrupted the flow of events, I've had to be more . . . overt in my actions."

"Why then, pray tell," Drake asked, "did you wait most of a year to act following this supposed disruption?"

Lucretia nodded at the comment. "When a change is made, sometimes the ripples of fate will resolve themselves. We see many possibilities, and try to avoid taking drastic action. But once I knew that the course needed to be corrected, I had to muster my power and find the most opportune time. And as they say: revenge, cold, and so forth. I won't deny there was also a personal motivation."

"And by correcting the course, you mean that I need to die?" Eastwood stood with his arms crossed, in full Cowboy Glower Mode.

"Yes. You were not supposed to survive Halloween. Our predictions showed that you would be consumed by your quest, and that Ms. Reyes here would enter the Underground only briefly before returning to her life. The ripples of change are compounding, and we're nearing the time when the changes will be irreversible, disrupting centuries of prognostication."

"So I was supposed to just go back to my life? And you're saying I only stuck with this because of him?" Ree asked, throwing a thumb at Eastwood.

"That is what our projections indicated. There is always room for individual choice, but the flows of influence, of ripples, all became clouded when Eastwood refused to die on Halloween."

"So somehow this is all my fault for saving his ass?"

"Yes, to an extent. But it is mostly Eastwood's fault, for turning away from making the sacrifice."

Eastwood harrumphed at that.

"And why should we care what your sisterhood thinks?" Ree asked.

Lucretia scoffed, maxing out her aristocratic air. "Not all of us care to live our lives so blithely careless to consequence."

Ree cracked her neck, holding back with the punching. She was also dead on her feet and had no desire to talk about anything wibbly-wobbly or timey-wimey right now. She wanted a huge-ass milk shake and then she wanted to go to bed.

"I think she's full of it and just trying to get off scot-free. Can we lock her up and go home now?" she asked.

Grognard chuckled. "I like the sound of that." He turned to Lucretia. "Screwed-up time or not, you're going to pay to fix my store. For your sake, I hope your sisterhood has deep pockets."

"That we do, but repairing a grown man's playroom is hardly my first concern. We must correct the flow, and it starts with Eastwood sacrificing himself. Once he removes himself from the river of time, the ripples will dissipate."

Eastwood's nostrils flared. "Like hell. What proof do you or your sisters have that you haven't just concocted a whole cosmology to justify pulling people's strings? I've heard of way less ridiculous worldviews used to justify killing people, and those were crap, too."

"I can prove everything, but Eastwood needs to die. If you stop me, others will come for him. And they will have far less regard for collateral damage than I."

"Yeah, because you've been a fucking surgeon so far," Ree said, gesturing to the ruined store.

"The point remains. My sisters will come. Charge me with whatever you want, have your trial at Market, do what you like to make yourselves feel better. But when the other Strega come, this city will burn." Lucretia crossed her arms and stood. "Take me where you will."

Grognard chuffed. "I don't have the time or give the shits to look after you. But I won't have to."

The big man went into the back room.

Ree studied Eastwood, saw him shifting, nerves showing through the exhaustion. *What if Lucretia was right?* She obviously wasn't, but if she was, would her sisters try to do some weird-ass time-travel shit to put things "right"?

Grognard returned from the back room with a frequent flier-size bottle of booze.

"Drink this, and then repeat after me," he said, pressing the bottle into her hands.

"What's this?"

"Drinkable geis. Drink and repeat after me."

Lucretia raised a painted-on eyebrow at Grognard, inspecting the glass.

"It's that or I get to babysit you here until next month's Midnight Market, where we can get the community together for a proper trial. And you don't want me for a babysitter."

"I imagine not," Lucretia said, opening the bottle. She shot the small drink, then looked back at the bartender.

"I, your name," Grognard said.

"I, Lucretia d'Fete."

"Do swear that I will deliver myself to the next Pearson Midnight Market."

Lucretia repeated the phrase.

"To answer for my crimes against Grognard and Eastwood, and will not seek to harm either of them, nor anyone in the Pearson Underground, until the trial is complete."

Lucretia repeated Grognard's words but added "except in self-defense."

Grognard nodded at the addition. "Lest I forsake my power forever."

The witch gulped, then finished the pledge. The air around Ree snapped into place, the world going perfectly still for a moment, like the sliders on a lock settling into place.

"Whoa," Ree said.

Grognard's mouth quirked into a slight smile. "That one took me a year to brew, two more to mature." He turned to Lucretia. "Now get the fuck out of my store. Don't ever come back."

The fate witch picked herself up and made for the door.

When she was gone, Ree slid around the counter and poured a healthy portion of scotch into four glasses and handed them out to the group.

"The rest of your liquor doesn't have geis power, right?"

"Nope. Just the power to compel people to drunkenness," he said.

Ree nodded. "Do you think Lucretia's shitting us?" Ree asked.

"It does seem rather convenient," Drake said.

"It'd be a great way to pull one over on us so she can get away with attempted murder without consequence," Ree said.

"And if her sisters do start making an appearance?" Drake asked.

Grognard raised his glass. The group toasted, then Grognard downed the whole thing in one go. He slammed the glass onto the bar. "Then we send them screaming back to their goth sorority house, one by one. I've been around awhile and known Lucretia for years, and this is the first I've heard about any of this crap."

Eastwood sipped from his glass, and breathed out, seeming to savor the scent of the old scotch. "If I am supposed to be dead, I might as well try to do something useful before the universe catches up with me." He turned to Ree. "And I can't think of anything better than trying to get your mother back from the Duke."

Ree gulped her own drink down, the potent vapors kicking her nose like a mule. It burned so good, all the way down.

Drake sipped on his drink, dignified even though she knew he was dead on his feet.

"Boss," Ree said. "Permission to clock out and go die for a while?"

Grognard nodded. "I'll give you a call when I decide what to do with this disaster zone."

"Anyone for milk shakes?" she asked.

Drake nodded.

"Good. That way I can give you your coat back."

"There's no rush. I intend to engage in some intense hibernation this week myself."

Ree nodded to Eastwood. "When we've rested up, why don't we pick a time and bring every rescue idea that doesn't involve taking Dark Side points so we can start fresh."

The cowboy nodded, still watching his drink as he swirled the clear caramel liquid around the polished glass.

Not supposed to be alive. That'd be a hell of a head trip, even though it's probably crap.

Ree grabbed her normal, not-fighting-monsters jacket, and nodded to the older geeks as they sat leaning against the bar, another bottle of Johnnie Walker Blue open between them. Ree and Drake took the office exit, since if Ree never saw another sewer tunnel in her life, it'd be too soon.

Once again, Ree was eternally grateful for the twenty-four-hour Burger Bin. The post-adventure milk shake had become a tradition for her (and for Drake, to a lesser extent), a fast and delicious war to dump hundreds of calories back into her system in a hurry.

Ree got her customary Shake of Victory, which basically involved throwing every single ingredient in the place into an industrial-strength blender and pressing Go.

Drake had vanilla.

They made their way out as soon as the drinks were ready, not wanting to press their luck in terms of the discretion of the overnight employees, who hadn't bother asking what the hell the two of them had been doing before walking in. Drake had put together a pretty good olfactory glamour to hide the sewer smell, but they still looked like rejects from a Victorian postapocalyptic rave. Plus, she still had a puffy shirt skirt instead of pants, which even bored high school Burger Bin employees had to think was weird.

They made their way to the park two blocks away. It was really just a triangle of grass, a few benches, and a couple of trees that filled up a street corner too small to hold a useful building. Ree took off her boots, laid her squidgy socks over the back of a bench, and walked on the dew-cooled grass. She took several long breaths, soaking in the texture of real earth, the crunch of the grass, and the scent of fresh city air. No walls, no dome, and, best of all, no fucking monsters.

And the whole time, a part of her brain circled back and back and back to Drake. The look he got when he reacted to the richness of the ice cream, the restrained flickers of unalloyed pleasure kept at the edges by his propriety, the curve of his arms, the bare skin of his neck.

Stay good, Ree. She stared at her milk shake, hiding in the exhaustion as they talked. The sugar and caffeine pushed her aches back, dimmed the headache a bit, but she still felt as wrung out as a pile of washboard laundry.

They'd found the right time of night to be ignored by the world, only a half-dozen lights visible from their spot in the park. It was a rich enough neighborhood to have a Burger Bin, was off the drop routes for the city's drug trade, and was populated enough to be a bad choice for muggings. Though she'd like to see someone *try* to mug the two of them, especially after the miserable night they'd had.

When both straws started making sucking-on-air sounds, they made their way through the four-AM empty streets to Ree's building. The same mischievous voice, rampaging on a sugar high, said on a loop, *Smooch him!* in the weird cousin to the "Shoot her!" line from *Jurassic Park*.

But her libido was not the boss of her. "You want I should bring your jacket back down?" Ree asked.

Drake waved off the idea. "No need. I wouldn't ask you to use the stairs any more than necessary. We will speak again soon."

Smooch him! the voice said again.

"Got it. Sleep well, Drake," she said instead.

Drake tipped a hat he wasn't wearing, an affectation he'd picked up from one of the many movies she'd inflicted on him.

The *Smooch him!* voice called out again as he stepped back to turn away. She wanted to watch him go but forced herself to tromp up the stairs and put herself to bed.

Dear self,

Go the F@% to Sleep.*

And so she did, dreaming aggravatingly pleasant dreams of Drake punctuated by Scott Pilgrim–esque nightmares of Gothic Lolita ninjas attacking Eastwood. Because that was her life now, like it or not.

Acknowledgments

First, my Epic Level +5 Radiant thanks to Adam Wilson, for his enthusiasm and wisdom in helping to shape the continuing adventures of Ree, Drake, and the gang.

To Meg White, for her thoughts on Lieutenant Wickham, as well as her stalwart support and tolerance of weekend afternoons in coffee shops.

To Sara Megibow, agent of awesomeness, for bobbing and weaving through the melee of publishing to keep me working and able to share these stories with the world.

To my readers, for the incredible honor they do me by engaging with my work, and for the unmatched, primal joy that comes from knowing that you've made people happy through storytelling.

To my fellow writers and storytellers, source of limitless inspiration, support, and camaraderie. You help make a lonely job far less isolating.

And most of all, thank you to the gaming community—dice chuckers, card-floppers, pewter painters, tabletoppers, console warriors, LARPers, game designers, everyone. Games and gaming have been a huge part of making me who I am and brightening my mood in times when I was low. This story is an attempt to reflect some of that brightness out into the world.

Michael R. Underwood
Baltimore, Maryland
November 2013

2ND EDITION ACKNOWLEDGMENTS

There are only minor tweaks here, similar to *Geekomancy* or *Celebromancy* – a substituted reference here, more inclusive language there, a quick polish with new formatting, and a fresh cover to give the book new life.

Some thank yous for this edition:

To CreativeJay for formatting and production.

To Deranged Doctor Design for the new cover.

To No Land Beyond for being my new home gaming store.

To Kim-Mei Kirtland for helping me build my career even as the world is overwhelming.

To the designers of the games that have inspired and entertained me in the past years. There are too many to mention here, but I'm so grateful to have games as a constant.

To everyone finding the series for the first time with these editions – you're keeping Ree and the gang alive.

Baltimore, MD
July 2022

Newsletter

Find out more about Mike's books, appearances, get bonus stories and more by subscribing to his newsletter at michaelrunderwood.com/newsletter

Hexomancy

Ree Reyes has been fighting to protect her town for a couple years now, using her Geekomancy to draw on her love of superheroes, movies, comics, and more.

When Ree's long-time nemesis Lucretia is finally brought to trial and found guilty for the deadly attack on Grognard's, the Geekomancer community breathes a collective sigh of relief. But Ree and her crew soon discover that Lucretia has three very angry, very dangerous sisters who won't rest until Eastwood—a fellow Geekomancer—is killed.

Ree agrees to serve as Eastwood's bodyguard, despite their rocky relationship. Along the way, she'll have to face a gauntlet of foes, hexes, curses. Plus the growing ache in her heart for a certain dimensionally-displaced gadgeteer.

For more adventures with Ree,
check out this short excerpt from *Hexomancy*

CHAPTER ONE

Cause I'm Leaving, On a Steam Cruise

Summer

The clock ticked toward 9 PM entirely too quickly as Ree raced to finish her closing tasks at Zombie Café. She appreciated Charlie giving her the shift, but it was hard to concentrate on overnight baking to-do lists and inventory when she was due in court in an hour. Especially when *court* meant "facing an enraged Hexomancer bent on murdering your erstwhile mentor and anyone who tries to stop her."

Fortunately, Ree's friend Priya was on hand to help keep her grounded. Ree's worrying mind could focus on talking with Priya, while her productive mind could work down the checklist the way she'd done five hundred times before.

Ree Reyes (Strength 10, Dexterity 14, Stamina 13, Will 18, IQ 16, Charisma 15—Geek 7 / Barista 3 / Screenwriter 3 / Gamer Girl 2 / Geekomancer 2) rolled out a length of plastic wrap over the d6 cupcakes, draped one side over her forearm, pulled the wrap taut, then pulled the other side up, cutting off a perfect square. She tucked the plastic wrap around the sides, careful not to smoosh the icing. It was a delicate art, and one she was glad to have not forgotten. She hadn't needed to do any baking at Grognard's, but it'd take longer than eight months for her to lose her edge.

Zombie Café hadn't changed much in Ree's absence over the last year. The twenty-by-twenty front room had well-worn tables and seats. Murals and paintings of rocket ships, superheroes, and dragons filled one wall, bookshelves and gaming merch lined the other, and between them, a cash-wrap overstuffed with collectible cards and pastries stood right in front of her.

And while Ree worked, Priya talked. Priya Tharakan (Strength 8, Dexterity 13, Stamina 12, Will 15, IQ 17, Charisma 15—Geek 3 / Professional 3 / Seamstress 4 / Steampunk 4 / Goth 2) was in "casual mode," an earth-toned scarf over a black top and slacks, her duster draped over the one table with chairs not already stacked up for closing time.

"The best thing was the music. Half of the bands were pretty much Mumford with Gears On, but whatever you call them, they were excellent," Priya said, recounting her time as an invited costuming guest on a Steampunk cruise. "This one band had ten members, including sitar, djembe, and banjo, and they actually had backstory to explain the fusion aspects—they were supposed to be the crew of an airship that traveled the world escorting dirigible freighters."

"That sounds pretty awesome. Did you grab their album?" Ree asked, dumping out the decaf coffee.

Priya pulled a CD case out of her purse and held it aloft like a prize. "Ta da!"

"Sweet. Can I borrow?"

Priya held the CD out toward Ree, a twinkle in her eye. "Keep it. I figured you'd want a copy, so I got two."

Ree took the case with excited reverence. "Best friend is best." The last month had been rough on the finances, hence her needing to take shifts at Zombie Café.

"So you're headed off to the catering job after this?" Priya asked.

"Yeah. The company has been losing customers, so I really need to take this one, or the boss is likely to write me off."

"What kind of events do you cater for?" Priya asked.

"Mostly private parties. Tonight is a soiree some muckety-muck lawyer is throwing for her friends and clients," Ree lied.

Every time Ree had to make shit up to cover for her magical life, it was like walking over burning embers. She'd learned to mute the pain, but it never quite went away. Other than her magic-world associates and her dad, only Anya knew about the magical world. The other two Rhyming Ladies had been kept in the dark to try to minimize risk. The result was . . . messy. Especially with Priya dating Drake Winters, one of Ree's constant companions in All Things Weird.

"What kind of food did they serve on the cruise?" Ree asked, turning the conversation back around, both so she didn't have to extend the lie, and because she was genuinely interested. It'd been harder to keep up with the Ladies with her whacky Urban Fantasy life, and Priya had put off an evening of engineering to come hang out, so she should get as much out of the short evening as she could.

Ree crossed a few more tasks off in as Flash-like a fashion as possible while keeping her end of the conversation going, converting nervousness over the coming trial into speedy efficiency. It was better than the alternative, which was to stop long enough to consider the long list of a million and one things that could go wrong at the trial.

After all, it wasn't often that a member of Pearson's magical community was tried by her peers in a massive underground cavern decked out like a mash-up of the Goblin Market and the Origins Game Fair. And that was precisely where Ree was headed, as soon as she got the café in ship shape and the clock struck 9.

The cashwrap clock read 8:47.

One thing at a time. Cupcakes first, doom later, Ree thought.

Life since Lucretia d'Fete had ruined Grognard's Grog and Games with a cascade of Hexomantic curses and several waves of monsters had been, in a word, *fucked.* Grognard didn't have the money to pay her for more than about five hours a week, which she spent throwing out trash, making major repairs, and mourning the tens of thousands of dollars of geeky merchandise that the events of that sucktastic Saturday night had destroyed, throwing an adamantium crowbar in the wheel spokes of her already shaky life.

Priya pulled her back to reality, gushing about the cruise. "And they've already asked me back to be a guest on the spring voyage, which is awesome. Being a guest pays a cool grand up front, plus room and board, and the chance to sell my merch and services. Two of these a year and I might be able to hire an assistant for the grunt work! And then I could make enough to finally pay off the Student Loan leg-breakers."

Ree stopped counting down the drawer, scribbled a note to keep her place, and looked up. "That's fantastic, Pri. And if you need a charming merch-booth minion, remember that I happen to love cruises." Ree punctuated the line with the biggest, most obvious wink she could.

"Yeah, but if you came with me, I'd come around my merch booth to find you playing *Pathfinder* with all of my customers," Priya said, referring to the one time (one!) that Ree had run merch for Priya at a totally dead one-day Steampunk con in Pearson.

"Hey, that was one time," Ree protested. "And that older lady bought a corset."

"Which was my only sale that day."

"Yeah, but even the hat and fascinator folks were having a crap day. There was nothing to be done with that festival."

"As evidenced by the fact that the con was a one-and-done." Priya packed up her bag.

"Okay, I should probably let you finish up, yeah?"

"Yeah, I'll need to book it to make the job in time. Thanks for coming by, and remember what I said about the cruise. I could use a vacation."

Ree scurried out from the cashwrap to give Priya a hug, and then locked the door behind her friend after she left.

Okay, what's left to do? she asked herself, scanning the room.

Eastwood had asked Ree to make it to market by 9:30, which wasn't going to happen. She was shooting for 10, and cutting corners wasn't going to help. Julio Reyes didn't raise no dumbass, and walking into the Midnight Market to square off against Lucretia at the trial was going to take every single bit of Ree's Geek-fu, and she wasn't about to walk in unarmed.

Ree booked it across the U-District, weaving among college students on the early stops of their weekend pub crawls on a sweltering summer night. Someone had scooped up a big bowl of Midwestern summer soup weather and dumped it on Pearson in a flagrant violation of the Pacific Northwest Climate Accord that kept her beloved city free of the kind of miserable humidity she'd learned to despise as a kid.

Adrenaline hurled her up the five floors toward the Shit-hole, her and Sandra's apartment. These days, the Shithole was much closer to earning its usually inaccurate name, thanks to Ree and Sandra's life erupting into matching fail-nados within a week of each other. Sandra's admin job at the dentist had gone poof when the practice got tanked by a malpractice suit, sending Ree's roommate back to the job market.

But there was no time to clean now (had there ever been?), so Ree dashed into the bedroom, thankful that Sandra seemed to be out once again. It'd been hard enough to keep her best friend and roommate in the dark over the last year, especially with Anya already knowing about magic and everything, and Priya dating Drake.

The having-a-crush-on-her-friend's-boyfriend thing didn't help either, but time was making that piece of angst slightly easier to digest.

Slightly.

Ree had laid out her arsenal on her bed before leaving for work, prepping ahead of time for a quick-change armoring session. Her old boss Bryan had agreed to let her pick up some shifts, as long as she didn't bring her magical business to Zombie Café. And that included the gear.

Clothes came first. She switched out her black-on-black work garb, stained many times over by frosting, coffee grounds, and steamed milk, and replaced them with her last remaining Urban Fantasy Adventure outfit—jeans (with only a few tears and holes), black undershirt, the quilted armor of convention shirts Bryan had given her last Halloween, and the magically-always-fitting-and-self-repairing buff jacket Drake Winters had given her on permanent loan. She tied her shoulder-length black hair up and back, pinning it with a Wonder Woman barrette.

She cleaned the shift's accumulation of crud off her old glasses, catching a quick glimpse in the mirror of how tired she looked. Puerto Rican heritage saved her from taking on the mime-esque chalky paleness that white folks got when they were wrung out, which she was sure she'd have if she'd taken more after her mom's Irish coloration.

And now the weapons.

Her Force FX lightsaber went from her purse (what Bryan didn't know couldn't hurt him) into the outside right pocket of the jacket, along with her *Deep Space Nine* phaser. She grabbed a rubber-banded stack of cards, flipped through the top to triple-check her selections, and then stuffed the sideboard into her left pocket. Along with those, she pocketed the last handful of health and stamina potions from her copy of *Descent*, a handful of dice (for ritual miscellany), and an external battery for her phone.

Such were the tools of a Geekomancer. Ree sometimes marveled at how little time had actually passed she discovered that she had the power to use her love of pop culture to do physics-defying magic, but if ever she needed those skills, tonight was the night. In her hands, the lightsaber and phaser were as real as they were to Luke Skywalker or Benjamin Sisko, brought to life by the collective nostalgia of fans worldwide.

The sideboard of collectible cards gave her access to one-shot effects—one card, one spell. And the phone was her own personal Power Ring, loaded with video playlists organized to grant specific powers. A quick rewatch of the opening to *The Matrix* could bestow limited Bullet Time powers, and smiling along with *Spider-Man* as he webbed his way across the city could make her a Friendly Neighborhood Spider-Gal—for a time.

And now it was 9:21. Ree double-checked everything and turned around in place to make really, *really* sure she wasn't forgetting a tool or weapon. She retrieved a slice of Turbo's pie from the fridge to nom along the way, one final power-up for the night's misadventures.

×✕⬡✕×

The doorman at the Midnight Market got obscure on her, which was cute. She didn't have time for crap, especially considering how many gnomes were still wandering Pearson's sewers. They'd been stirred up last month and hadn't settled down.

"What's the first appearance of Karnak?"

Since she'd used a copy of *Fantastic Four* #45 just last month during Lucretia's attack, she rattled off the reference as easily as her phone number.

Three bolts and locks slid open, and Ree entered the Midnight Market, leaving behind the smell of sewage that had gotten entirely too familiar to her this last year.

She nodded to the bald doorman and strode down the hall, which was suspiciously low lit. Was this their version of flying the flag at half-mast? Three of the people who had left Grognard's that night never made it home: Tomas, Alexi, and Siobhan.

The Midnight Market filled the room, more stalls and booths this month than she'd seen in months. Were they all here for the trial? Ree'd never been to a Pearson Underground trial, though Eastwood and Grognard had gone over the details with her what seemed like a hundred times.

Kiosks, booths, and wandering traders spanned twelve rows deep, hand-painted signs erected at the open walkways between booths. Ree passed comics-backlist sellers, action figure gurus, 3D printers, miniatures sellers, and costumers.

Farther down the lane was her traditional neck of the woods, where Grognard's cart would be parked at the corner of Geneva and Talsorian. The cart had been lost in one of Ree's all-too-frequent adventures in the sewer, but the space was still occupied by the man himself. Grognard was dressed in his Saturday best, a stain-free shirt with a leather jacket.

Grognard aka "Just Grognard" (Strength 15, Dexterity 10, Stamina 15, Will 18, IQ 15, Charisma 10—Geek 7 / Collector 4 / Geekomancer 3 / Brewmaster 5) was a living statue of a man, built thick with muscle, head shaved clean. His beard was immaculately kept, and for the first time at market, he was packing. It was a halberd rather than a gun, but considering Grognard topped 6'2" and two hundred fifty pounds, he usually didn't need anything in the weapons department to feel safe.

Beside him, shifting his weight side to side like a pendulum of nerves, was Eastwood. The former Console Cowboy (Strength 11, Dexterity 14, Stamina 14, Will 18, IQ 18, Charisma 7—Geek 8, Astral Cowboy 4 / Geekomancer 5 / Thunderbolt 2) stood just a few inches taller than Ree, with a well-worn trench coat (yes, even in summer) over a blazer and slacks. Ree'd never seen Eastwood in slacks. He still wore his weapons belt slung low like the Cowboy he had been and remained.

Eastwood had been on edge since that night at Grognard's, but tonight, he was more put together than she'd ever seen him. His beard was freshly trimmed, his hair shampooed and combed. He looked, frankly, like he was going to court. But he was still off—pale, slightly red around the eyes.

Ree gave the chin nod of companionable silence as she walked up, joining the two men. They returned the nod, and Grognard pulled out a flask from his jacket and held it out to welcome her.

"Care for a sip?"

Ree looked at the flask. "And this is?"

"Critical Hit ale. Figure we can use every bit of help possible."

"You okay?" Ree asked Eastwood.

Eastwood snorted back snot by way of answer. "No. I caught the frakking flu. I might as well be a snot elemental." He pulled a handkerchief from his blazer and blew. And kept blowing.

Ree grimaced and took a sip from the flask. She felt the tingling of magic, felt the universe slide into the booth next to her and offer a tipsy high five, saying, *You got this! Woo!*

Whatever was coming, she felt just a tad more prepared. "Everything set?" she asked.

"As set as it can be," Grognard said. "Drake's not here, and neither is Wickham. But Talon, Chandra, Shade, and Uncle Joe are; that's more than enough testimony to back our story. Plus," he said, reaching into his jacket again, "we have this."

The brewmaster pulled out Lucretia d'Fete's handwritten note that basically admitted her guilt. In a U.S. court, this would be an open-and-shut case. But this was the Underground, and she hadn't seen thousands of hours of *Law & Order: Pearson* to give her the confidence of familiarity. She imagined Eastwood and Grognard as cop and lawyer for *L&O: Pearson* and chuckled.

"What's that for?" Eastwood asked.

"Just imagining something weirder than our life. Perspective is handy," she said.

Eastwood sneezed, dramatically undercutting his badass demeanor. "Don't go daydreaming too much, kid. Eyes on the prize."

Ree held the flask out toward Eastwood. "You need some of this? Maybe Crit your way out of that flu."

"I get the vaccines, I take my old-man vitamins, and still, this frelling thing." Congested, Eastwood's gruff voice sounded dangerously close to that of a Muppet.

Ree felt the hairs on the back of her neck go up, Spider-sense-style, and she turned to see Lady Lucretia d'Fete walking down the aisle. Lucretia (Strength 9, Dexterity 13, Stamina 11, Will 17, IQ 15, Charisma 14—Strega 9 / Hexomancer 3 / Seamstress 3) held her head high, her makeup perfect, black hair styled in a complicated updo maintained by a half-dozen spikes and needles.

She was followed by Sven Carlssen, her frequent sellsword bodyguard. Sven was loaded down like a warrior in an Obsidian RPG—a half-dozen weapons visible over his coat: bow, crossbow, sword, daggers, another sword, and a fuckoff-size Bat'leth on his back.

If it were anyone else, Ree would snicker at the preposterousness of wearing that many weapons all at once. But she'd crossed blades with Carlssen. If he was wearing all of those weapons, she was betting that he was in a position to use them.

Lucretia walked past the corner of Talsorian and Geneva, head held high, actively refusing to meet Ree's or her companions' eyes.

A smart woman would let it sit there, would allow Lucretia to pass without incident.

Ree felt like being dumb. "You ready to take a fall, Lucy? NordicTrack here isn't going to save you from the long arm of geek law."

A hand gripped her arm, squeezing ever so slightly too tight. It was Grognard. She restrained a snarl and watched Lucretia miss half a step, the comment slipping past the woman's cool demeanor like a dagger under the folds of plate.

That won't be the only sting tonight—you can bet your ass, sister, Ree thought, tossing her angry thoughts at the Strega.

"Harassing her isn't going to help our case," Grognard said.

"Yeah, but we were all thinking that, right?" Ree looked to her boss and her former mentor. Both shrugged, grinning.

"That's what I thought."

And so they went to court.

About the Author

Michael R. Underwood is an author, podcaster, and publishing professional. His books include space opera *Annihilation Aria*, the Ree Reyes *Geekomancy* books, the Stabby Award finalist *Genrenauts* series, and Born to the Blade (written with Malka Older, Cassandra Khaw, and Marie Brennan).

Mike has been a bookseller, sales representative, and was the North American Sales & Marketing Manager for Angry Robot Books. He is also a co-host of the actual play show Speculate! and a guest host on the Hugo Award-finalist The Skiffy and Fanty Show.

Mike lives in Baltimore with his wife, their dog, and an ever-growing library. He also loves geeking out with games and making pizzas from scratch.

Follow Mike on Twitter @mikerunderwood.

You can support Mike's writing at patreon.com/michaelrunderwood